Our Wallflower Queen

THE MEN OF PSYSPECOPS
BOOK 2

KAMERON CLAIRE

SNUGGLE WHORE PRESS, LLC

PSYSPECOPS

OUR
WALLFLOWER
Queen
KAMERON CLAIRE
USA TODAY BESTSELLING AUTHOR

Dedication

To all the Witty, Wicked & Wild Readers...
Never let them silence our Witty Tongues,
Never let them shame our Wicked Needs,
Never let them stop our Wild Deeds.
If it harm none, do what thy will!

Praise Kink

BDSM terminology is vast, varied, and often up to interpretation. For the purpose of this book, these definitions apply to our submissive and her Dominants…

Praise Kink is using/receiving affirmation—whether verbal or through physical touch—to elicit/derive sexual pleasure. It's not simply giving compliments, although that is part of it, but it's using positive and kind words to give verbal approval for a task attempted and well-done.

ENTES TUERE
PUNIRE IMPIOS

Chapter One

LETI

EVEN THOUGH IT'S SATURDAY—A day where most people sleep in and girls my age nurse hangovers—for me, today starts like any other day.

My alarm goes off at six am. I roll out of bed, put on a pair of yoga pants, a sports bra, and a baggy t-shirt—all from my sister's athletic wear line, Krush Kruisers—and am jogging the neighborhood of our Barrington Hills estate by six-fifteen. Most days, this is a solitary experience because you can't see my neighbors' houses from the road, and with the exception of the occasional passing car on their morning commute, I never run into anyone.

So, when an older model tan van passes by, I take notice—even though I also dismiss them as workmen of one kind or another. Maybe they're pool cleaners or carpenters or masonry specialists? Most of the houses in this area are less than twenty years old, but bored housewives remodel all the time.

It's when the van passes again and then pulls over at

the end of the lane that I start to worry. Slowing down, I pull my phone out of my yoga pants. At the same time, the van makes an erratic U-turn and drives right at me. I turn back to my house and run as fast as possible. I'm a little over a mile away from home with no driveways or trees to dash into, which means I'm utterly defenseless when the van screeches to a stop beside me and I'm tackled and thrown into the ornate bushes lining the road.

A man twice my size spins me on my back and grabs hold of my left wrist. When he moves for the right one, I fight with everything I have, kicking and flailing and trying to move his massive weight off me. Screaming for help, he lands a well-placed backhand to my cheek. Instantly, I fall limp—my bell thoroughly rung as stars and birdies and jewelry box ballerinas dance through my darkening tunnel vision.

He throws my temporarily boneless form over his shoulder and tosses me mercilessly into the back of the van.

The vehicle pulls another erratic U-turn, sending me and the big guy across the floorboards.

Glancing around through unfocused eyes, I see the silhouette of a man sitting behind the steering wheel with a woman staring at me from the passenger seat.

"Let me go," I moan right before the scary man, with malice twisting his features, shoves a rag into my mouth. I try to push off the floor, but he holds me down face first and binds my wrists with ease. When he moves to my ankles, I flail, kicking and screaming around the foul cloth shoved in my mouth.

"Dope her," the woman growls from the front seat.

He sits on me, easily pinning me with his strength, and with a quick prick, the world goes dark.

I COME to with a horrific headache, the likes of which I have never before experienced. My eyes are swollen and puffy, and my mouth is thick and dry even though the dirty rag is gone. My body aches, but it's only when I try to wipe the gunk out of my eyes that I realize I can't move my arms or legs.

Through haze-filled eyes, I take in my dank surroundings. I'm lying with my arms and legs tethered to a bed frame. There's a window on one wall, but the curtains are drawn, and outside of the sliver of sunlight shining through, I have no idea as to what time it is. The room is dark, dusty, and filled with stale cigarette smoke and a rancid odor I can't place.

A normal person would start screaming right now, hoping someone outside would hear and rescue them, but not me. I've gotten through life by keeping quiet and waiting for people to forget about me.

The door swings open, and the scary man who tackled me fills the doorway.

"You're awake." His voice is gravelly, like a lifelong

smoker who inhales three packs of unfiltered cigarettes a day.

I try to ball up into the fetal position, but it's not going to happen with my arms and legs stretched wide.

I don't have to ask what they want—I know what they want.

Money.

With my father's enormous bank accounts, I'm sure they think they can get some, too.

I say nothing.

The scary man walks toward me, opens a switchblade and, without a word, cuts my T-shirt from the top, ripping it open.

"Please don't," I finally rasp, unable to stop the tears from rolling down my cheeks.

I don't want to be raped. It's not necessary for them to achieve their financial goals. "You don't have to do this. Tell me what you want, and I'm sure we can work something out."

Behind him walks in the woman from the van. She sits at the edge of the bed and stares at me, shaking her head. "Don't you have something to say to me?"

I stare back at her, searching my memory for some clue, but I don't recognize her. "What would you like me to say?"

"An apology would be nice. Although, I don't think I've ever heard you apologize to anyone, so I guess I'm not surprised that even in your current predicament, saying 'I'm sorry' wouldn't cross your mind."

I have no idea what this woman is talking about, but if an apology works, I can do that. "I'm sorry."

"Are you? I don't think you are. I think, like everything else in your perfect little life, you see nothing wrong with what you did."

I drop my eyes, my throat tightening in a sob. "I'm really, really sorry."

"I think we should strip her," the man says near my head.

"Tell me why you're sorry." The woman holds up her hand to signal the man to hold that thought and raises her eyebrows in my direction.

"I didn't mean to hurt you."

The woman's eyes narrow on me. "Oh my god, you're such a fucking brat that you don't know why I'm angry. I knew you were self-absorbed, but I had no idea your narcissism ran this deep."

At this moment, I realize this isn't about me.

It's not about my father's money.

They think they have Pip and have no idea who I am.

Nobody would ever call me self-absorbed. Half the time, people don't know I exist, and the other half, people think I'm some wallflower to be walked on and taken advantage of—which in some ways I suppose is true.

I've been hiding from people most of my life. Where my sister is the first one to jump on a table and dance for the cameras, I'm the one standing behind the curtains, trying to make sure nobody sees me.

Quiet as a church mouse—that's what they say.

The woman's eyes scan my face, as if she's cataloging

every freckle, every imperfection, and then her eyes grow wide. "Epi?"

I steel my facial expressions, so as not to give away my little secret. "Yes?"

"Say my name."

Doing everything I can to channel my sister's bratty, sarcastic, beautifully unafraid persona, I click my tongue and say, "Kidnapper."

She stares at me for a couple of seconds and then looks at the man, giving him a chin tilt.

He flashes me a greasy, gut-churning grin and puts his hands on my hips, bunching the top of my yoga pants and shoving them down to my ankles.

The woman stands to look down at me. "Spread her legs."

All the bravado I attempt to muster masquerading as my sister flies out of me as he slides his hands between my thighs. "God, please no! Please don't!"

"Where is your birthmark?" Her eyes come back to mine, anger simmering in them. "Who the fuck are you?"

My only response is to cry. Coupled with whatever drug they gave me, a series of bone-cracking sobs only make my head pound harder.

"Son of a bitch!" The woman stomps out of the bedroom, screaming profanities as she goes.

The man continues to leer at me, his eyes creeping, touching, and violating every inch of my skin. He slides his hand in between my thighs again, squeezing hard enough to leave a bruise. "I'll be back for you later."

Then he does something unexpected and loosens the

straps on my wrists. "There's a bathroom, and as long as you keep quiet, I won't gag you. Besides, it gets me hard when my prey runs and fights."

He's chuckling as he walks out of the bedroom and slams the door shut behind him, a series of locks turning from the other side of the weathered wood panel. I don't dawdle, pulling up my yoga pants and removing the straps on my legs. I curl into a ball and take in my surroundings. They think they have Pip, or at least they did, and now that they know better, she's in danger.

I hop off the bed and check the window, only to find that it's boarded up from inside and outside. Then I run into the bathroom, finding one small window above the shower that I couldn't fit my foot through. I rifle through all the bathroom vanity drawers to find them empty. Not even a toothpick or a spool of floss, not that I would know what to do with either of those. I come back into the bedroom and look around. Besides the dirty mattress on a rickety frame and a chair in the corner, there's no furniture in this room.

No drawers to rifle through, or pictures to pull off the wall and smash over somebody's head, or sheets to wrap up in.

True despair settles into my chest as my adrenaline wanes. I crawl onto the bed and pull my knees to my chest as I listen to the distorted voices beyond the door.

Ten, maybe fifteen minutes later, the series of locks is disengaged. Jumping off the bed, I sit on the chair and curl myself into the tightest ball possible.

The man walks in first, grinning when he lays his

eyes on me. I had no idea a man's smile could be so sinister.

Rife with malice and promises of violence.

The woman walks in behind him, shaking her head. "A twin. Leticiana Krushner, Epiphany's fucking twin! How did I not know about you?"

I shrug, but I know how. I've spent my entire life living in the shadows, doing everything I can to not cause attention. I am my sister's polar opposite, and even though we are mirror copies of each other, we are absolutely nothing alike. She's everything I have never had the courage to be. She's loud and proud and in front of the cameras, smiling and flirting and talking—everything people gravitate to.

Me? Not so much.

"Are you worth any money to your father? I mean, I couldn't find anything via a casual search about you online. It took my technical skills to dig you up. Why is that? What are you hiding from?"

I don't answer her. Instead, I stare and keep my mouth shut, like I have my entire life.

"Answer me!"

"I'm sure my father will meet whatever ransom demands you have." The words rush out of me.

She sighs. "We'll soon find out. You're going to be our guest for a couple of days."

Another man walks into the room, tall and thin, but covered with the kind of sinewy muscle models or swimmers have. He's attractive by high society standards and nothing like the other man who scares the absolute hell out of me. He drops a box on the floor as the woman walks out of the room.

"We'll have a camera trained on you at all times, so I suggest you be good and you might survive this." Her voice trails off as she walks away, leaving me in the room with the two men.

The guy who looks like a frat boy—his eyes narrow as he looks at me. Then he turns to the other man who hasn't taken his eyes off me once. "I wonder if she's as much of a cock tease as her sister?"

"I hope she's a fighter," Scary Guy rasps.

Frat Boy smiles. "You like getting bloody, don't you?"

Scary Guy grabs his dick. "Fuck, it makes me hard thinking about it."

"You are a sick man." Frat Boy walks out, chuckling down the hallway.

Scary Guy points to the box. "Sorry it's not gourmet, but it'll keep you alive for a couple of days." He pulls the door shut behind him, closing us in the room together.

I drop one foot to the ground, preparing to run, and he flashes me a vicious smile.

"Rabbit, rabbit, rabbit." He lurches forward as I jump up to crawl over the bed, but he catches my ankle and pulls me to a stop. Again, he flips me as if I weigh nothing, throwing me to my back, his body covering mine. "Where are you going?"

I struggle underneath him, turning my face away from his hot breath on my cheek. "Get off me!"

He jerks his hips forward—making sure I understand

how hard this makes him—and puts his mouth over my ear. "I can't wait to fuck you, but until then..."

Bouncing off of me, he grabs my yoga pants and rips them off of my legs again. This time he also grabs my underwear, leaving me completely bare from the waist down. "I want you sitting in here, naked, waiting until I get back. Who knows? Maybe you'll miss me, but I hope not. I really fucking hope not. I hope you sit here thinking about how much you hate me, how much you want to hurt me, and how much you want to fight me taking every little shred of your innocence."

He walks out with my yoga pants and panties in hand, lifting them to his face and inhaling deeply. "See you soon."

The door slams behind him and once again the locks are engaged. I count four in total. Two are deadbolts, but the keyed locks are inside the room, which means I have no way to keep them from reentering whenever they want. They were obviously thinking ahead because the door swings out versus in, so the momentary thought I have about putting the chair in front of the door to barricade it is rendered moot. I have no way to protect myself —no weapons to use. I sit and wait, listening as muffled voices talk down what seems like a long, endless hallway.

After a period of relative silence, there is movement on the locks. Once again, I put one foot on the ground, knowing that being agile is my only defense. The door swings open and the woman walks in, her face distorted and flushed with anger. She has a phone in her hand, the speaker engaged.

It rings three times before my father speaks. "This is Walter Krushner."

She screams into the handheld. "Why didn't you tell me I had the wrong daughter when we spoke this morning? Is this one even worth thirty million?"

My eyes widen. Thirty million is a lot for most people, but not my father.

To my surprise, Pip's voice comes through the receiver. "Let my sister go, you son of a bitch!"

The woman looks surprised, but a calm smile takes over her face and her demeanor changes instantly. "Epi, Epi, Epi. I had no idea you had a twin. You've never mentioned her. Should I do to her all the things I was going to do to you?"

My father's voice cracks, a rare display of emotion I haven't seen or heard in ten years. "Don't hurt her. Please, we'll pay whatever you want."

Having my father speak seems to make something within the woman snap.

"I wasn't talking to you!" she screams and steps aside as the big man rushes into the room, hauling me out of the chair by fisting a handful of my hair.

I can't help it.

I scream.

He backhands me, sending me sprawling across the dirty mattress.

The woman looks at me, and for a moment, her features soften. Then she waves her hand, and the man leaves me to walk past her down the hallway.

She stands in the doorway, glaring at me. "She looks

just like you, and yet, she's nothing like you, Epi. At first, I thought it was the difference between your public persona and the real you. It's the lack of a birthmark on her leg that clued me in. Do you know, she never once told me I was calling her by the wrong name? What kind of sister would risk torture to keep you safe when you've never publicly acknowledged her existence?"

She closes the door, locking it behind her. Time drags on and I lay here, my body aching, my face throbbing, and I hear very little from the other side of the door. Then a vehicle rolls up to the house, followed by a car door slamming shut. Between the spaces between the boards nailed to the window, I see nothing but trees and the front of the tan van, making it obvious I'm not in some normal, run-of-the-mill neighborhood with houses stacked on either side of each other. For all I know, I'm in a trailer in the middle of nowhere.

The TV comes on at the same time as more car doors slam shut. I run to the window and see the tan van pulling away from the house. I don't know why, but I exhale the breath I've been holding, the tension in my shoulders subsiding the tiniest bit.

Something tells me I'm alone in the house, the TV on merely to disguise the lack of voices on the other side of the door. Regardless, I'm utterly helpless. Digging through the box the frat boy dumped on the floor, I find a couple of sandwiches, bags of chips, crackers, fruit roll-ups, and bottled water. Pretty much everything a twelve-year-old boy on a camping trip would be excited about having. Although I don't think I'll ever be hungry again, I am parched and desperate to wash from my mouth the foul remnants left behind by the rag. The seals on the water bottles are intact, so I crack one open and take a drink, wondering if and how I will survive this.

What is this doing to my family?

My father and sister sounded genuinely distressed on the phone, which gives me a bit of solace, I guess. After my mother died ten years ago, the three of us handled her passing differently. Our father threw himself into his businesses, growing an already successful empire into a multi-billion-dollar conglomerate. He never remarried, but I have seen women slip out of the house in the morning. I've never taken the time to introduce myself because I know they won't be around for long.

My sister handled our mother's death by not dealing with it. She hid herself from me and everyone, eventually glomming onto opportunities that took her far away. She's modeled and has been a spokesman, but now she has her own brands and a YouTube channel with over five million followers.

With no one to commiserate with, I was left alone. But I couldn't be like my sister. I couldn't abandon my father, even though he neglected both of us. So I adapted the best I could, making sure I was there to take care of him from the shadows. When he offered to send me to the best boarding school money could buy, I declined, choosing to attend a private school within driving distance of the house. I threw myself into my schoolwork, and while Pip traveled the world with private tutors, I advanced in my classes to graduate a year early. I started college at seventeen and attended Loyola University Chicago because, once again, it was within driving distance of the house.

I even joined my mother's sorority after I turned eighteen my sophomore year—Kappa Kappa Gamma. As the daughter of a third-generation Kappa with a billionaire father and a three-point-nine grade point average, they offered me membership despite my lack of social skills or interest in living amongst them to do all the traditional sorority/fraternity things.

I remember the morning I told my father I was a Kappa Kappa Gamma like Mom. He never looked up from his paper, but I noticed how he flinched when I said *like Mom*. Then he smiled, congratulated me, and told me to let him know when he needed to send in a check. Two minutes later, he left me to finish breakfast by myself.

Even after graduating with honors and joining Krushner Industries as a junior portfolio analyst—identifying holes in our investments and prepping presentations specifically for him—I can't get more than a couple minutes of my father's attention at any given time. I'm not sure if it's because I remind him of his dead wife, or if it's because he resents us for being left behind after she died.

Maybe he never wanted to be a father?

Who knows?

He's never been deliberately cruel; he just wasn't there. The desperation in his voice, and the fury in my sister's words—that's what sticks with me as time ticks by and I'm left alone with no clue as to what awaits me on the other side of this door.

Actually, that's BS.

I know what awaits me, because the scary guy told me.

He's going to beat me.

He's going to rape me.

And if he does all that, he will surely kill me.

My lack of defense, coupled with the fear of what's coming, is bound to drive me insane.

ENTES TUERE
PUNIRE IMPIOS

Chapter Two

REESE

I WAKE up to my phone ringing from one of the handful of numbers authorized to alert me.

"Yeah?"

"Krushner, Kilo-Romeo, Epiphany and Leticiana. Grab your team, find out everything you can, and meet me and Lee's team at the father's Barrington Hills estate in one hour. I hope none of you had late nights."

"Roger." I hang up the phone. One thing I love about my boss, Victor, is that he is a man of few words. Direct and to the point. His motto is *get the fucking job done* and the only reason why I can handle working for him.

I roll out of bed with my cock at half mast, brush my teeth, and take a piss, before I open my bedroom door and yell down the hallway, "Rise and shine, fuckers! We got a job."

There's grumbling coming from Caiden's room.

Except it's not morning. It's nearly noon. But it is also Saturday, and we were up late last night dicking around with our vehicles downstairs and contemplating a visit to the club tonight.

Jumping in the shower, I take a quick three minutes to rinse off and really wake up before donning my suit, which is the only thing I don't like about this job. I'd rather live in tactical gear or joggers, but there are a few things in life that require a jacket and tie.

Meeting a client for the first time is one of them.

The other is a night at the club.

Sliding the end of my silk tie through the Windsor knot has a Pavlovian effect on me, my dick hardening for all the wrong reasons.

"Down boy," I grumble, thoughts of the last time I wore a suit and the things I did with my tie to a willing female causing my blood to stir.

Walking out of my room, I catch Soren in the kitchen, pouring himself a cup of fresh coffee. He's already dressed, most likely because he was up hours ago. He greets me with a raise of his mug and then walks over to his bank of computers along the wall. "Who am I looking for?"

"Epiphany and Leticiana Krushner."

"Okay. Why?"

I cast him a look that tells him how stupid his question is. "Dude, you know Victor and his stance on brevity. I have no fucking idea, but I'm going to assume kidnapping as that seems to be our forte as of late."

"It's better than babysitting pop princesses and pampered princes."

I nod and sigh. "Ain't that the goddamn truth?"

"All right, let's see what I can find."

I grab a cup of coffee and stand over Soren's shoulder while I look up the address Victor texted me. I calculate it'll take us twenty-five minutes to get there and we need to leave in ten. I yell over my shoulder, "Hurry up, asshole!"

From down the hall, I hear Caiden respond, "Go fuck yourself, Reese."

I chuckle—he really isn't a morning person—and return my eyes to the computer monitors. On one screen, the program Soren designed to scour public records pops up dozens of windows with pictures of Ms. Epiphany Krushner.

"Fuck, she's hot," I mutter before taking a sip of the dark, aromatic brew. Soren became a coffee snob after we separated from the military, so we only drink the best at home.

At the office is another conversation.

Soren nods. "Yeah, and she's pure trouble. Owner of Krushner Kosmetics and Kruisers Athletics, she's got five million followers watching her every move. She's a social media influencer and worth a couple million annually."

A collage of photos of her in a bikini pop up on the screen. "Is she also an Instagram model?"

"Looks like she's done a bit of everything, to include a few international incidents with some of the richest men in the world. They took these pictures on an Arab prince's yacht off the coast of Abu Dhabi."

"Fuck," I slide my hand down my face. "Another pop princess."

"Leti—which is the only name I can find her by—I had to use special tools to find online. She's not searchable via any of the normal channels."

"No shit? Has her information been scrubbed?"

I hear Caiden approach from behind, cursing under his breath. "Fuck, is this a suit and tie event?"

He's wearing the standard gear to include a tight black Under Armour T-shirt and black cargo pants. I don't have the strength to answer his dumb ass. Instead, I throw my arms out and show him what I'm wearing.

He turns around and curses the entire way back to his bedroom. "Putting on a tie is going to make my fucking dick hard."

I laugh, because yeah.

"Not necessarily scrubbed, but she has little to no digital fingerprint. Here she is." Pictures of a much more subdued Epiphany pop on the screen. Graduation photos, sorority pictures, company headshots—nothing that speaks to her personality or experiences.

"Twins?" I ask, a bit surprised.

"Identical, born seven minutes apart." Soren's fingers continue to fly over the keyboard, entering commands into one of a dozen programs he's designed.

"What about the parents?"

Soren clicks a few buttons and more windows open up on his multiple screens. "Walter Krushner, owner and CEO of Krushner Industries, amongst a few dozen subsidiaries. Widower, fifty-two years old, he never remarried. He's self-made, mostly. Married his college sweetheart, an affluent woman by the name of Chrissy, who died in a head-on collision a little over ten years ago."

"Is there lots of money in play?" I toss back what's left of my coffee and glance at my watch, realizing we are going to be late.

I'm gonna kill Caiden.

"I'd say so. He's worth a few billion. Last ranked number three hundred eighty-six on Forbes' top four-hundred richest people in the world."

"No shit?" I say again.

"What are we doing?" Caiden walks up behind me in his suit, adjusting his cock in his pants.

"Seriously, man?" I grin.

He narrows his eyes. "You know putting on a tie gets me hard, just like it does you."

Soren stands and shakes his head. "You two are no better than animals."

"Yeah," Caiden and I say at the same time.

Caiden walks to the front door, nodding at Soren. "I'll throw our gear in the truck while you pack your whiz bang tools."

Soren types a couple of commands and then undocks his laptop. Sliding it plus a couple other things into a bag, he hoists it onto his shoulder. "I'm ready."

The three of us function like a well-oiled machine. We've been together for fourteen years, out of the military for three, working for Victor for the whole time. We were PsySpecOps in the Army and met after they recruited us out of our career fields for the special duty.

PsySpecOps soldiers aren't like other soldiers. Hell,

we aren't even like other special ops units. We're a cross of Spec Ops, Intel, EXO, Cyber, and psychological warfare, to name a few.

Imagine if Chuck Norris, MacGyver, and B.F. Skinner all jerked off into a test tube and then impregnated Wonder Woman. That's us.

That's a joke, but not a far-fetched one. We're like what you get when you take somebody who has special forces training and then put them through the FBI Quantico behavioral sciences program. It takes us two years to graduate training and requires an eight-year commitment. After undergoing multiple psychological and behavioral tests, they placed us in groups of three, damn near guaranteed to be compatible in every way.

Caiden, Soren, and I are scarily in tune with each other to include our likes, dislikes, and preferences in all things—even sex. And I know we're not the only ones, because we've seen other guys from our unit at our favorite local playground—The Access Club. It's never been confirmed, mostly because we don't talk about it, but there's got to be something to the psychological profiles they build on us that correlates to being the kind of men who prefer sharing the same woman.

I jump into the passenger seat while Soren climbs into the back with Caiden at the wheel. "You got our shit?"

Caiden throws the Suburban into gear and nods. "All the basics. We'll have to go to the garage for the fun shit."

I glance at the address on my map. "Take 90 west to Sutton."

"Roger."

"Did Victor mention who else was going to be on the job?" Soren asks from the backseat.

"Yeah, Lee's team."

"I'll send them what we have." Soren pauses as he sends out a mass message to all of our phones, to include Victor's. "I'm pinging both of the women's phones. One is on the property while the other one is about a mile away on a residential street. We might want to stop when we get close."

"Whose phone is a mile away?" Caiden asks.

"Leti's."

Twenty minutes later, we're talking to Lee, Case, and Porter as they drive to the house. They are two minutes behind us, so it's no surprise they pull over with us at the location where Soren says Leti's cell phone signal is the strongest.

We all climb out of our vehicles and search the sides of the road.

"We got tire tracks here." Lee points out a set performing multiple U-turns in the middle of the road.

"Call her phone. Maybe she's that one person who leaves her ringer on?" I suggest.

Soren pulls out his phone and dials the number. We wait with bated breath, but sure as shit, the phone starts ringing in a bush closest to Caiden. He jumps down the little gully and takes a few steps forward, way too far off the road to have fallen from her pocket.

He picks it up and turns to us with a look on his face that does not bode well for Ms. Krushner. "We have signs of a struggle. There are numerous broken branches on this little landscaper's dream. The rest of the shrubs are in perfect condition."

I nod, the clock officially starting on Ms. Leti Krushner. Most kidnappings that aren't resolved within forty-eight hours end in tragedy. We don't have a lot of time to dick around. "Let's get to the house."

Victor is waiting for us outside when we pull up. I hand him Leti's phone and give him a thirty-second rundown of what we found and then shut my trap once all six of us are standing in front of him.

"Here's what we got. Mr. Krushner, the girl's father, received a phone call around six-forty this morning demanding a ransom for Epi Krushner. The perpetrators said they would call later with more details, but wanted to give him a heads up so he had time to amass the thirty million they are demanding. Mr. Krushner called the FBI, his lawyers, and then me."

I glance at my watch. "It's one o'clock now. Why are we just getting here?"

Victor slides his eyes my way. "Because I only received a call ninety minutes ago."

Caiden interjects. "Evidence points to Leti as the one who is missing, so why are they asking for Epi, which I assume is short for Epiphany?"

Lee asks at the same time. "Has the father contacted his other daughter?"

Victor sighs. "Apparently, the father doesn't know Epi's current phone number. I figured you'd have it by the time you got here."

Soren nods, typing something on his iPad. "I got it right here, and it is on the property."

"No shit?" Victor raises his brow. "That's good news, I hope. I get the impression the father doesn't have the closest relationship with his daughters, although he does seem genuinely upset. Lee, you and your team are on Epiphany. Reese and team, you've got Leti. Let's get inside and see if we can get at least one of the two daughters secured."

We walk into one of the nicer houses I've ever been in, with a grand staircase greeting us in the middle of a giant marble foyer. There's a lot of activity going on to the right, which appears to be an office where the FBI are setting up a bunch of equipment. Soren sneaks in behind us, while I take the opportunity to introduce myself to the lead agent, ensuring I piss him off and distract his men at the same time. It only takes thirty seconds for the lead agent to dismiss me, telling me to go fuck myself in the most politically correct manner possible.

I hate working with the FBI, but it's a necessary evil sometimes, and it gives Soren a chance to tap into their recording equipment. I rejoin the rest of the men in the foyer while Victor talks to the father, giving him the number Soren provided for Epiphany.

Taking in the decor, the house has a very cold and staged vibe to it. It looks like something out of a magazine and not something lived in. Everything is white and gray and even the wood has a muted tone to it, giving it a museum quality. There are no pictures or any other indication a family lives here.

Seriously, hotels have a more welcoming warmth to them than this house.

Lee leans in, keeping his voice low. "What have you guys been up to?"

I cup my hand and shake it like I'm jerking off. "A lot of this."

He chuckles. "Yeah, us too."

A few minutes later, Epiphany Krushner comes running into the house from behind the staircase, wearing what I can only describe as an itsy-bitsy bikini. The woman is beyond beautiful, stacked like a centerfold, and curvy in all the right places.

"Holy shit," I hear Caiden whisper while someone else coughs.

"Epiphany Krushner?" Victor steps forward to acknowledge her.

"Who are you?" Her eyes drift over all of us, then go back to him. If she's self-conscious in any way, she hides it well. I would think running into a room full of large men would be intimidating fully clothed, but this barely dressed hellcat doesn't seem affected.

"I'm Victor Townsend, owner of the Townsend Security Agency. These men are members of my team."

"Where is my father?" she snaps.

"He's in his office with the FBI and his lawyers." How Victor keeps his cool is beyond me. I'm already over her attitude and I've only spent thirty-seconds with her.

The put-out attitude drops as confusion crosses her face. "Wait. What? How long ago—"

At that moment, her father walks out of his office.

She immediately goes on the offensive, attacking the man who looks wrung out. "When did you get a phone call asking for ransom?"

"Let's go into the library." Mr. Krushner grips her upper arm and escorts her across the foyer. We follow Victor, leaving the FBI behind.

Soren takes the opportunity outside of the FBI's line of sight to grab a seat at a small desk nestled behind the door, sliding his laptop and other gear out of his bag while the Krushners fight with each other and then with Victor and Lee. It's obvious as I stand back with my team that she's not thrilled with the idea of being placed in protective custody. Talk about babysitting a pop princess. I'm glad it's them and not us. I'd much rather be on the team assigned to track and extricate the kidnapped victim than play bodyguard to an unwilling body.

Even a body like hers.

"Daddy, I have a shoot this Wednesday," she whines, and I catch Lee and Case both flinch. Under any other circumstance, I'm sure her attitude would make them hard. They like bratty women. They like to make them submit. And they like to do it together.

Yes, we've seen them at the club, so we know their sexual preferences are similar to ours, even though they enjoy women who challenge them, while we prefer to pamper our reserved ladies and bring out their wild sides.

Now she's in Lee's face, counting down her many obligations.

He, on the other hand, remains stone faced, which I think only makes her madder.

"This is entertaining to watch," Caiden says under his breath.

"It really is," I agree.

The phone in Mr. Krushner's office rings, and he jumps from his seat to run out of the library.

Victor, Lee, and I follow him, standing in the doorway of the office as the FBI hits a button. The kidnapper has realized at some point that they have the wrong sister and they are pissed. The sound of Leti screaming at the same time as flesh-on-flesh contact echoes through the speaker causes my blood pressure to rise.

I can't stand to see a woman manhandled unless it is full-on consent, and even then it makes me antsy. I watched my mom's boyfriend smack her around a couple of times, and then I came at him with a baseball bat, breaking his nose and fracturing his cheek.

I was twelve.

Shaking it off, I tap into the deep, dark recesses of my brain where everything is numb.

Memories from my past don't haunt me here.

Emotions don't prevail.

This is a job.

These are our clients.

Male or female, we will do our jobs and bring them home safely.

Lee bumps me on the shoulder to bring me back to the here and now, and we move as a unit to the library, closing the door behind us.

Lee turns to Victor. "We have to get her out of here. Now."

Victor nods. "Absolutely. The sooner the better. What did you see on the trace?"

We all turn to look at Soren, who shakes his head. "Whoever this is, they're pretty good. The signal is bouncing all over the world. It doesn't sit in one place long enough to leave much of a fingerprint, but I'll get it. It's going to take me a bit to narrow it down."

"The location on Leti's phone stopped moving at six thirty-three this morning, so they could be three hundred miles from here by now. The first phone call was within minutes of the kidnapping, but this call came from a location where the kidnappers can mask themselves," Lee points out.

"Okay." Victor takes control and hands out assignments. "While Soren's doing his thing, Reese—your team is on extraction. You should go to the garage and get everything ready. Lee—you, Case, and Porter have the princess. Good luck."

I chuckle and slap Lee on the back before turning my attention to the ones and zeros flying across Soren's screen. She's difficult to find, which means whoever took her is no amateur. Soren is one of the best hackers in the world—recruited by all the three-letter agencies, and yet he chose to stay with us. His brain is wired differently—a certified genius—but if he's having a problem getting a lock on the kidnappers, they've got to have a decent amount of skill themselves. "Something tells me this is going to take longer than expected."

Lee raises his brow. "Unless you kill whoever the fuck is behind this during extraction."

A treacherous smile spreads across my lips. "One can only fucking hope."

"Don't get shot," Lee says as he walks out the door.

"You're the only one who gets shot," I call out, landing a below-the-belt blow to Lee, who turns to face me with a murderous glint in his eye. Oh, man, if we weren't in a client's house, we'd already be rolling around on the ground—I know it. Lee was shot three years ago while on a mission, and that injury plus the resulting surgery got him sent home with a medical discharge. Once one member of the PsySpecOps team is retired, they are all effectively retired in the career field. Case and Porter could have stayed in the Army and cross-trained, but they also opted to separate.

We had a similar situation when Caiden blew out his knee during a firefight. They sent him home for surgery and extensive rehabilitation, decommissioning our team for six months. Our separation date was on the horizon and when Victor Townsend—retired Colonel Townsend, commander of the PsySpecOps 8th Division—heard we were on the fence about reenlisting, he made us an offer we couldn't refuse. The Townsend Security Agency only recruits and hires ex-PsySpecOps teams, which maintains our team dynamics, even though a couple of guys who live down south come in on an as-needed basis, usually to team with Victor himself.

Lee grumbles as he walks out of the room, "Fuck off."

Caiden chuckles beside me. "I love those guys."

ENTES TUERE
PUNIRE IMPIOS

Chapter Three

SOREN

I CAN'T GET a good lock on the signal the call came from, but I've triangulated it to a fifty-mile radius that is two hundred miles from here. We're heading that way to get as close as possible until they call back.

As I'm packing my bag, Case runs in with a small Netgear hub in his hand. "Her ex-IT person designed her this *scrambler*. Do you want to check it out?"

"Absolutely." I tuck it into my laptop bag.

"Are you leaving?" He glances around, presumably for Reese and Caiden, who are upstairs checking out Leti's room for any potential clues—although we don't expect to find any. From all accounts, Leti is an innocent bystander who happens to be an identical copy of the real target. They premeditated none of this with her in mind.

"Yeah. We're heading to the garage. I think I have a lock on Leti southwest of here near Peoria. I'll look at this *scrambler* while the guys are packing the tactical gear."

"Are you going with them for extraction?"

I slide my eyes to the side to look at him, the question grating on me, even though I don't think he means anything by it. Although we all have the same training, we don't all excel in the same things. I, for instance, am skilled in all things tech. The other guys could do much of what I do, especially with the tools I've created, but it's not easy for them like it is for me. Meanwhile, hand-to-hand combat isn't my strong suit. Don't get me wrong, I can kill a man just like the rest of them. I have the training, but for Reese it wouldn't take five seconds, while for me there might actually be a scuffle. With this group of men, it's a bit embarrassing to know I'm the weakest amongst them.

"Yeah, the signal's too erratic to not be tracking her constantly," I say dryly.

He nods, the look on his face apologetic although no words come from his mouth, and hands me a cell phone. "Can you make this seem like it's working, but take it offline and route all the traffic internally to us?"

I laugh and take the phone from him. "Is she giving you hell already?"

"You have no idea."

"Yeah, but you guys like that. Chicks with a ton of attitude make you hard." I glance over at him.

Rolling his eyes, he grumbles, "You have no idea."

"They are beautiful, aren't they?" I pop out the SIM card and slid it into a small handheld decoder I modified years ago. Then I open an app on my phone, something I also designed that routes any SIM card I program to an internal messaging service on all of our phones. This entire setup takes me ninety seconds.

"Yeah, they're beautiful." He sighs and takes back the phone. "Thanks. You guys be careful out there."

I nod, hoisting my bag on my shoulder. "You'll hear from us when we have something."

"Same." Case fist bumps me and is out the door.

I'm the last to leave the library, and I can feel a half-dozen FBI eyes trained on me, eyeballing my bag of tricks. I doubt they'll find the trace duplicator I put on their equipment, but if they do, I already have the MAC address and will backdoor it if need be. Yes, that would be a felony, and yes, I could face jail time if caught, but I don't worry about things like that. Not with Victor at my back.

I give the boss a head nod and exit the property, climbing into the backseat with Caiden and Reese already situated in the front.

"All good?" Caiden asks, as he puts the SUV into gear.

"Yep." I pull the little *scrambler* device out of my bag to inspect it. They broke the factory seal, but that's not a huge surprise. I often take commercial items and retrofit them to serve my purposes. It's called garage engineering.

"What's that?" Reese asks, his big body turned around to watch me.

I shrug. "I guess Epiphany has an ex-IT guru. They designed this device to help her broadcast while hiding her location. While you guys pack our gear, I'm going to do a bit of reverse engineering."

Reese frowns. "IT guru? Could that be why—"

"That's what I'm thinking. It certainly explains the erratic signal and why I can't get a lock on it," I say, interrupting his thought process.

We pull into the garage under Townsend Security Agency headquarters located in downtown Chicago. I have no idea how Victor afforded this little gem of a building smack dab in the middle of one of the busiest and most congested cities in the country, but he did, and it is nice. If the neighboring office buildings had a clue as to the amount of ammunition, explosives, and tactical equipment housed in this building, they would be nervous.

Very, very nervous.

As the guys head for the cages, I walk to the tiny clean room Victor installed for me right after coming to work for him. Not that I need a clean room for this, but it's kind of my space to work in, and I know where everything is. I remove the four small screws and crack open the case, finding a simple tracker glued to the lid. A quick inspection shows me what I expect to see—a micro-board with a few crossed wires interrupting the outbound signal by sending it through an additional board programmed to encapsulate the originating IP packet.

Simple and straightforward, but this tracker is a surprise that is definitely not supposed to be here.

The tracker itself is also a relatively simple GPS module capable of broadcasting a signal any time they plug the Netgear hub in. That is its only fallibility. It has no power source. Of course, attaching one would have made the tracker more obvious, or at least the scrambler device itself, bulky and suspicious.

Prying the tracking chip off the lid, I turn to my shelf of goodies and pull down a device with input and output wires. I power up my laptop, connect it to one side and bring up a Unix shell to input a series of commands. Because I don't know if this tracker is being monitored in real-time, I don't want to apply power and have it broadcasting my location any longer than necessary. At the same time, I need it to connect long enough to backtrace the signal and zero in on where this ex-IT guru is. Hopefully, it lands smack dab in the middle of the current area I've triangulated outside of Peoria, solidifying my original intel, which—let's be honest—is half-assed at best.

I apply power to the chip and watch my laptop as the tracker turns on, orientates itself, negotiates its lat/long coordinates, and then broadcasts them to a masked IP address.

"Oh, fuck you," I mutter under my breath, working my magic to unmask said address.

In the background, a map pops open, drilling down every eight seconds to a location northeast of Peoria, dead center of my grid.

Thank god!

"I got him!" I yell loud enough for the guys to hear me.

"You do?" Caiden pops his head in.

"Yeah, damn near dead-center of my original guess."

"Of course it is. No one ever doubted you." He grins

at the same time the door swings open and Reese steps inside.

"Do you know where we're going?"

"Yep." I throw my software on the giant screen in the room and zero in on the rusty top of a trailer in the middle of nothing, the closest house two acres away. Placing a tag on it, I send the lat/long coordinates to their phones. "X marks the spot."

Reese smiles. "It sure the fuck does. Let's go."

I remove power from the tracker and pack all my shit, just in case we need it. "Grab the portable generator."

"Got it," Caiden says over a Snickers bar stuffed in his mouth.

Seeing the food, I remember none of us have eaten and I'm starving. "Drive-thru on the way?"

NOT EVEN AN HOUR after leaving Mr. Krushner's property, we have a lock on Leti and are driving like bats out of hell down the interstate. I polish off the last of my sandwich, crumbling the wrapper and stuffing it back into the bag. "We should call the other team."

Caiden hits a button and the phone rings over the car's audio system.

"Yeah?" Case says.

"Hey. We've got a lock on Leti's location and are heading there now. Meanwhile, I took a quick look at this little Netgear hub, and while they programmed it to scramble the originating IP address, it's also got a little GPS tracker inside of it. Whoever's on the other side of this knows where it is at all times, and if Epiphany has been carrying it with her, it's been giving somebody her location within half a mile or better every time she plugs it in."

"Interesting. That explains why they knew she was at her father's residence," Case says slowly.

I don't think he understands how great this discovery is, and I'm getting more excited the more I talk about it. "It's better than interesting. It's because of this hub that we know where we're going, since it popped hot at the location I'd triangulated off the phone call."

They meet my excitement with silence. "That's fantastic, man. Who's in the car with you right now?"

Reese and Caiden exchange a look and then Caiden says, "What's up?"

At the same time, Reese says, "Yo."

Another pregnant pause before Porter speaks. "The designer of that hub is a woman, Claudine Humphrey— an ex-employee of Ms. Krushner's. From the story Epi told us, she's most likely a hostile ex-employee with an ax to grind."

"A woman? That's not the typical M.O. of a kidnapper." Caiden glances at Reese and then back at me through the rear-view mirror.

"No, but something she said has me thinking." Case goes on to explain something about a business opportunity Epi passed on and the dollar amount asked for as ransom, which was raised significantly higher once the kidnappers realized they didn't have Epiphany, but a doppelgänger.

"Did you ask the client about this?" I ask, because they are right, the ransom amount is too weird.

$142,368,212.72 weird.

"No, not yet," Case says.

Porter follows up. "If it's a woman behind this, she has to have male partners. Even though the twins aren't much to handle, how many women do you know who could wrangle another woman to the ground and then inflict bodily harm?"

Reese responds dryly, "There are some out there."

Another pause before Case says, "Damn, I've never popped a woman before."

"They bleed just the same as men," Reese says.

Caiden glances at me and I nod, knowing that Reese has done that thing where he quickly compartmentalizes things, sinking his psyche into a cold place where everything goes numb. He doesn't relish the idea of killing a woman—hell, none of us do—but he will if it comes to that.

Dear god, please don't let it come to that.

"Whatever it takes," Case retorts.

Reese nods. "Exactly. We'll call you guys tonight, after it is done."

Caiden disconnects the call and checks the navigation unit on the truck. "We've got about two hours of driving and three hours until sunset. How do you want to play this?"

Reese sighs, his gaze fixed on the road beyond. "We'll get within distance and then use the drone to get a visual. But we won't move in for extraction until after nightfall."

"There's a possibility this chick has cameras all over her property. I mean, her skills are good enough." I pull open my laptop and launch a debugger.

Caiden looks at me through the rearview mirror. "What are you working?"

"I can't monitor the tracker's originating end without alerting her we are on the move and heading in her direction, but I'm thinking I might be able to use the MAC address from earlier and track her that way."

"You think she's on the move?" Reese turns in his seat to look at me.

I shrug. "It's possible. Unfortunately, the only way I could grab her location was by broadcasting my location like I was Epi. If she's as good as I think she is, she would have traced right back to us in downtown Chicago, nowhere near the Krushners' residence. So, do we risk alerting her to our approach, or go in blind and potentially miss her?"

"See what you can do, but the last thing we want to do is alert her to our approach."

"Roger." I go back to my computer and we all fall into this comfortable silence, the miles ahead of us stretched out, giving us a quiet-before-the-storm vibe. We have no idea what we are walking into, which has me thinking about background information on Ms. Claudine Humphrey.

It's like Reese is reading my mind. "Have you pulled up information on this IT chick?"

"Yeah. Not much here via the normal channels. She's got a LinkedIn profile and an Upwork account advertising herself as a web designer and a contract IT specialist. She's from the area and graduated high school in Plainfield. No college degree, but a bunch of technical certificates—so self-taught, maybe? Blue-collar parents, both still alive. Father draws a medical pension at fifty-four. Mother still goes to work every day stocking shelves at one of the big box stores. One older brother, alive, married with two kids. One older sister, deceased. She herself has never been married."

"Fairly benign," Caiden says.

"Yeah. Let's see if I can find what they have scrubbed from the Internet." My fingers fly over the keyboard as I launch a program I wrote many years ago that mines the deep, dark recesses of archived data, looking for keywords I specify. I start with her name, then cross-reference it with Epiphany Krushner.

Hit after hit after hit pings my computer. I launch a series of photographs, my eyes bugging out of my head. "Holy shit."

"What?" Reese spins around in his seat. I turn my laptop so he can see. "Damn."

"What?" Caiden barks, clearly annoyed he can't look because he's driving.

"Epiphany Krushner and a bunch of other models changing clothes during a photoshoot, I'd guess. It looks like Ms. Humphrey might have been infatuated, taking discreet photos from what appears to be a camera in a bag. The shots suck, but they show enough."

I close the pictures and read a few data trace logs. "It looks like she bugged a lot of Epi's stuff and has been keeping tabs on her for a while. How long ago did the client say she fired her?"

"Six months," Caiden says.

"I wonder why she took so long to make her move?"

Reese shrugs. "Maybe she was grooming the right henchman. What about her known associates?"

I chew on the inside of my cheek, something I do a lot when I'm deep in thought. "Looking those up now."

ENTES TUERE
PUNIRE IMPIOS

WE'RE PARKED HALF a mile down the road from the property. The sun has dipped below the horizon, and an hour ago, we parked our drone on top of the dilapidated mobile home. There's one beater parked outside the front door, a Honda Civic circa 1985, but otherwise the property is quiet. There's been no activity coming in or out of the house, and besides a very loud TV playing inside with the occasional sound of a carbonated drink popping open, there's nothing.

I mean *nothing* nothing—eerily so—and it makes me nervous about what we're going to find when we get inside.

Under normal situations, we would have informed the local authorities and coordinated a search and rescue effort, complete with a warrant, but people don't hire us to do things normal. We will get in and out of there with as little bloodshed as possible, but if blood does need to be spilled, Victor will deal with it later, as he always has.

"Are you ready to go?" I glance at Soren, who is strapping his vest in place.

He nods, pulling out his Glock. I put the Suburban into gear and creep down the road, approaching the property with our lights off. We haven't seen another vehicle out here since we parked, so this is a very desolate area. I park the truck on the road in front of the driveway and we exit the vehicle with absolute stealth. Reese and I will take the front while Soren covers the back.

I test the door handle, finding it unlocked, and after making eye contact with Reese, we push through the front door to surprise some kid who is high as a kite, judging by the amount of smoke floating below the ceiling. A bag of chips and a can of cheap beer fly as he jumps to his feet and attempts to run. Reese has him on the ground within two seconds, has him secured within ten, and is marching him out of the house as I continue down the hallway, clearing the kitchen and opening the back door for Soren before turning and clearing a bedroom full of computer equipment and another with a made bed. This is not a home. This is a safe house, or torture shack, as the case may be. The bedroom at the end of the hallway is the one that concerns me. There is a series of locks on the outside—deadbolts easily turned from my side of the door, but also a series of padlocks.

I murmur to Soren. "Grab the bolt cutters and a blanket."

He holsters his weapon and nods, jogging out of the house.

Gently, because I have no idea what's waiting for us

on the other side, I rap my knuckles against the door. "Leti? Leti Krushner?"

Nothing and nobody responds.

Soren comes running in behind me with Reese by his side and a pair of bolt cutters in hand. I make quick work of the locks and then open the door slowly, my eyes scanning the dark room. There's a dirty mattress and a tattered recliner in the corner, a bathroom to the left with a tub and no shower curtain. Since the door swings out, we don't have to check behind it as we enter the room. Soren drops to his hands and knees, looking underneath the bed. He looks up and shakes his head. There's only one other place somebody could hide in this room, and that's behind the chair wedged into the corner.

If she is not there, then she's not here, and we are starting all over again.

I stand on one side of the chair and look over the top at a huddled mass of naked flesh. "Leti?"

She responds with a whimper, the first sound I've heard since we entered the room.

"Leti Krushner? I know you're afraid, but we're here to help you. We're going to move the chair now."

She responds by curling tighter into herself, her hair covering her shoulders and her face, her long legs tucked so far underneath her chin that I can't imagine it's not painful.

Reese pulls the chair away, exposing her to our eyes. She's naked from the waist down, dirty, but not bloody from what I can see. I crouch to her level, but keep my hands to myself.

"Leti, can you look at me?" Soren hands me the blanket.

She shakes her head as her response.

"Leti, I have a blanket for you. Can you stand up so I can wrap it around you?"

She peeks at me through her hair, a pair of jade green eyes like her sister's shining despite the darkness. Beautiful, except one problem—one eye is bloodshot.

Her voice is strained as she asks, "Where is he?"

"Who?"

Shaking her head, she curls back into herself, resting her forehead on the top of her knees.

Reese uses his most gentle voice. "There's no one here besides us, Leti. My name is Reese. My partner with the blanket is Caiden, and standing beside me is Soren. We're here to take you home."

She turns her head and peers up at him and then back at me, eyeballing the blanket in my hands. Like a scared little squirrel reaching for a hand-fed nut, she wraps her fingers around the edge of the blanket and pulls it to her. "I'm naked."

"We have clothes in the car, but we need to get you out of here first."

"Don't let him get me." Her voice cracks and it fucking breaks my heart. I don't know what this motherfucker did to her, but if I get an opportunity to put a bullet between his eyes, I'm fucking taking it.

Reese says, "We're not going to let anyone touch you ever again."

I stand and take a couple of steps back, still holding

the blanket. "How about I hold the blanket out for you and when you stand up, none of us will look?"

She nods and lets go of the blanket. I unfold it to its full width and turn my head, waiting for her to stand. It takes her a full minute, which makes me worried about how long she's been sitting like that and what damage they have done to her. She turns her back and grabs each end of the blanket, wrapping it around her, but it didn't take a second for me to see the bruises on her upper thigh.

Visceral rage courses through my veins as my eyes snap to Reese. I know he saw it, too, by the look on his face.

"Can you walk?" I ask her, noticing she stumbles when she takes one step forward. This could be something as simple as being curled tight in a ball for hours on end or it could be something more. Considering the bruise on her thigh, dear god, I hope it's not something more.

She brings her head up for the first time, her hair falling back, revealing a myriad of cuts and bruises on her beautiful face. Her lip is split, her ocular bone and jawline on the left side bruised, her eye bloodshot and there's a small cut on her cheek bone—presumably from a ring.

"My legs are numb, tingling with pins and needles," she says weakly.

I nod. "If you would permit me, I'll carry you."

She hesitates before nodding, pulling the blanket even tighter around her. Reese pulls the chair out further, giving me plenty of room to swoop her up into my arms. Following Soren out the door with Reese bringing up the rear, I carry her to the truck and place her gently in the backseat. "We need to secure the house, but I'm locking you inside and will only be gone for a minute. Okay?"

She shakes her head desperately. "Please don't leave me."

I look at Soren. "How about my partner stays with you while Reese and I lock up the house?"

She looks at Soren and must find him less intimidating, because she nods while tucking her feet underneath her ass.

I wordlessly convey to Soren everything he needs to know and nothing he wasn't thinking on his own before shutting the door. Reese and I walk back to the house, and only once I'm positive we're out of earshot do I let the curse words fly. "Motherfucker. Motherfuckers! If I get the chance, I'll kill that motherfucker."

Reese nods, his jaw clenched tight, but says nothing.

"Did you see—"

"Yeah, I saw it." Reese keeps his eyes forward.

"We've got to get her to a hospital."

"Yep."

"What are we going to do with this asshole?" I motion to the lump hog-tied on the dirt near the Civic.

"Honestly, I don't think he knows a thing. I asked him where the rest of the crew was and he said they left hours ago."

I kicked the piece of shit in the stomach to make myself feel better. "Hey, asshole. Tell us what you know."

He coughs and sputters, "Man, I don't know nothing. Some chick paid me a thousand bucks to babysit her house. All I had to do was hang out until she got back. She left me with all the beer and weed I could fucking handle and the only rule was I'm not allowed to go into the back bedroom, and if anything went down, I'm to call her."

"How are you supposed to call her?" Reese asks.

"She left me a phone, man."

"Where did she find you?" I ask.

"Craigslist."

"Are you fucking kidding me?" I glance at Reese, who seems just as surprised as me. "Did you have any idea that there were thugs for hire on Craigslist?"

"Anything is possible on the Internet." Reese shakes his head.

"I'm not a thug, man. I'm a house sitter."

"Fucking stoner," I snarl, my lips curled in disgust. "Do you have any idea what was in the back bedroom?"

"No, man. I haven't heard a word from the back there since I got here. Besides, I don't have a key to get in there —not that I would have if I did—because I'm a good house sitter and I do what I'm told."

I shake my head, a recurring dose of disgust for my fellow man making its weekly appearance. We can't take him with us. Leti is way too fucking traumatized for that shit and I'm positive Reese is thinking the same thing.

"Where are the keys to your car?" Reese asks.

"They're in my pocket, man." He looks up at us through half-lidded eyes.

Reese cuts the zip ties around his ankles and hauls him to his feet while I begrudgingly reach into this guy's pocket and pull out his keys. "Go back into the house. Wait for the owners to come home. Meanwhile, we're taking your keys."

"In other words, don't fucking leave." Reese smacks the guy on the back of the head before cutting off the zip ties holding his hands behind his back.

The stoner stumbles forward a couple of steps and then turns to face us. I brace for him to make a move, but he doesn't have the balls to try something. "I just go inside?"

Reese walks inside and comes out with a cell phone. "Is this the phone you are supposed to call her from?"

"Yeah, man."

I shake my head. This guy is worthless. "Give me your wallet."

He reaches into his back pocket and pulls out a billfold made of duct tape. I'm sure some stoner girl made it for him one night and the more I look at this guy, the more sorry I feel for him. He has no idea what the fuck he's involved in. I open the wallet, pull out the thousand dollars and his ID before handing it back to him.

"Hey man, that's my money."

I pocket all of his cash and ID. "Now you're more inclined to stay here and wait for the people who hired you so they can pay you."

We lead him up the rickety steps and shove him into the house, closing the door behind him.

Then Reese pulls out his phone and calls Victor.

"Yeah?" Victor says softly.

"We got her," Reese says dryly.

"Any casualties?" I can hear Victor scooting out of his chair, the legs sliding across the marble floor, his footsteps on the move.

"There's no one here except for some house sitter who had no idea what was going on."

I add. "We need you to call the local L.E. to take care of this guy. Meanwhile, we've incentivized him by taking all of his shit."

"I can do that. Hold on, I have the father here." Victor put us on speaker, which limits what we can say instantly.

"How's my daughter?" Mr. Krushner asks.

Reese and I exchange a look. This is the hard part because you never know what is going to trigger somebody. Do we tell him the truth and get his permission to do what we know needs to be done? Or do we sugarcoat it, putting the client's conscience at ease?

"She's traumatized, but to what extent, we don't know. We think it's best we take her to a hospital to be examined and have any evidence collected."

There's silence at the other end of the line, and I don't think this guy is stupid in any way whatsoever. His voice is shaky when he comes back. "She won't go to a hospital. Neither of my girls will. The last time we were in a hospital was when their mother died. However, I have a private physician that will go wherever I tell him to go. Are you bringing her home?"

"We should discuss that, Mr. Krushner." Victor says

calmly. "The kidnappers are on the loose and considering they took your daughter within a mile of your home, I am not sure this is the most secure location for either of them. Granted, we could make it secure, but I don't know if you want to bring that into your home."

"You're right. Of course you're right." Mr. Krushner sighs, sounding thoroughly exhausted and relieved. "Can I talk to my daughter?"

We're walking back to the truck. "Yes, sir. Standby one."

I swing open the passenger door to find Soren red-faced with Leti's toes tucked underneath his thigh. "Leti, we have your father on the phone."

Her eyes grow big and she shakes her head.

Over the receiver, Mr. Krushner says, "Lambchop? It's Daddy. Are you okay?"

Something about his words breaks loose a dam within her, and she starts sobbing, tucking her head into her blanket.

Reese takes the phone off of the speaker and walks away with it pressed to his ear. "Perhaps we should give her a few minutes in a safe space to decompress."

...

"Yes, sir, we will do that."

...

"Yes, sir. We will do that, too."

...

"Who?"

...

"Roger." Reese slides the phone into his pocket.

"What did he say?" I ask, my brow furrowed.

"With Claudine and her accomplices on the run, he's bringing in two guys from Tennessee so they can run the groundwork while we're securing the clients."

"Who?" There are only a few he could call who are not already on his payroll, and I'm betting I know who they are.

"Paddy from Ken's team and Bastion from Stiles' team."

I grin because I was right. "Right on. They like getting bloody."

He nods. "That's what I remember too. Meanwhile, we need a place to go."

"Soren will know the closest and safest location nearby."

We returned to the car, surprised to not only find her feet tucked underneath Soren's thigh, but his hand resting on her calf. She seems considerably calmer with him touching her, and I wouldn't be surprised if she was starved for physical contact.

The right kind of physical contact.

"We need a location," I murmur to Soren at the same time Reese speaks directly to Leti. "We'd like to take you to the hospital."

Her head snaps up, a wave of panic taking over her features, her words coming rapidly. "No. No, hospital. Why do I have to go to the hospital?"

Reese speaks very slowly and calmly. "We should have your cuts and bruises attended to and also have any evidence collected, should we need it for a trial."

She says nothing for a long time, staring at him like a deer in headlights. "I'm sure I look worse than I am, but there's no evidence to collect."

I swallow the rage bubbling inside of me. "What about the bruises on your legs?"

Her eyes drop to her lap, and her voice grows small. "They're just bruises. Yes, he stripped me and yes, he touched me, but he didn't rape me, so there is no evidence to collect. I never got a chance to scratch him or pull his hair, so I have none of his DNA on me." Then she mutters so low under her breath that if I didn't have amazing hearing, I wouldn't have heard her at all. "Or inside of me."

Sighing, I exchange a look with my partners. I don't want to push her any more than necessary, so I take a deep breath and relax my shoulders, willing my anger away—for now. "We need to get you somewhere safe. Are you aware you were not the intended victim?"

"Yes. They thought they were grabbing Pip."

"Although I advise against it, we can take you home if you want," Reese says.

"No." Her head snaps up again. "I don't want my father to see me like this."

Reese nods slowly and looks at me and then at Soren. "Then we will take you somewhere safe."

"What about my sister?" Her green eyes bounce from Reese to me and back again.

My phone beeps with a safe house location thirty minutes from here. I nod at Soren, who sent it to me, and then give Leti a gentle smile. "Your sister is with a team in an undisclosed location. Until we apprehend the perpe-trators, you and she will remain on lockdown in separate locations for both of your safety."

Leti presses her lips together, and then winces, presumably from the pain of the cut on her lip. "Is she... Is she okay?"

Reese nods. "She's worried about you, but otherwise, she's fine. Do you want to talk to her?"

She puts her head back down on her knees. The woman is flexible and twisted like a pretzel. "Maybe after I shower and feel a bit like myself again?"

"Then we'll go." We close her door, Reese and I exchanging a look that conveys all the rage and sorrow we feel for our client, who is as gentle a human being as they come.

ENTES TUERE
PUNIRE IMPIOS

Chapter Five

LETI

I DON'T KNOW how to describe the feelings I have.

Relief. Gratitude. Anger.

I've never wished another person physical harm in my life, but I want nothing more than for the men who saved me to find the man who threatened to do horrible things to me and hurt him—badly.

Perhaps I should feel blessed he never got to carry out any of his threats. I mean, of course, I am thankful they saved me before it was too late, but every time I close my eyes, I see his face. And I don't think the fear will go away until I know he's dead.

We drive into downtown Peoria amongst row after row of cute little ranchers inhabited by the blue-collar workers of the lower middle class. The house we pull into the driveway of is quaint with a small, postage stamp yard and blue shutters on the windows.

"When did we get this house?" Caiden asks.

Soren, the man who has been sitting next to me with the gentlest touch I've ever felt, responds. "We bought it two months ago. Finished construction on it a couple of weeks ago."

The man sitting in the passenger seat, Reese, shakes his head. "We are smack in the middle of suburbia. Are we sure this is safe?"

Soren closes the laptop that's been on his lap since we climbed into the truck. "This thing has the security of the White House, but only fourteen hundred square feet to manage. We'll be fine here."

He points to a keypad on the garage door. "The code is seven-six-five-three-pound and when we get inside, there will be a garage door opener on the bench."

Reese jumps out of the truck and opens the garage door.

Caiden drives us in and waits until the garage door closes behind us before shutting off the engine. He then turns around in his seat to look at me. "How are you holding up? Are you ready to take a shower and change into some clean clothes?"

I try to give him a warm smile, but it doesn't reach my eyes. "Yes, please."

"One of us will run out while you're showering to grab food. Is there anything in particular you would like to eat?"

I shake my head. "I'm not hungry."

He flashes me a sad but sympathetic smile. "We understand."

When we exit the garage, I have Caiden on one side

of me and Soren on the other. Both reach out to touch me and then drop their hands back to their sides, as if they're not sure they should. Honestly, right now, their touch would comfort me, but I have no idea how to tell them that. Instead, I wrap the blanket tighter around my shoulders and scurry through the door Reese holds open into the back of the house.

The house is cozy on the inside and has a new car smell to it. It's obvious we are the first ones to be inside after they remodeled it, the smell of fresh paint and chemical cleaner strong.

"Come this way." Soren escorts me to a room down a long hallway. He opens a drawer in the chest and pulls out a pair of brand new sweatpants and a sweatshirt. "I'm sorry these haven't been washed, but it's either this or you have to wear some of our clothes."

"Could I wear your clothes?" I blurt out, much to my surprise.

He brings his eyes to mine. "If that is what you want."

I glance at my dirty feet on the carpet. "I would like that, as long as it's not an inconvenience."

"Not at all, Leti." Soren rubs his neck and looks around the room. I'd guess he's as socially awkward as I am, judging by the way he fidgets. But how can that be when he's one of the three men to rescue me? "There's soap and shampoo in the shower, fresh towels on the sink, spare toothbrush and toothpaste in the drawer—most everything you need for tonight. Tomorrow, if you have specific things you want, I will get them for you."

He turns to walk out and then looks over her shoulder. "You can close the bathroom door, but I would prefer you don't lock it—in case you need us. I will go get your clothes and put them on the bed and then close the door to give you privacy. You're safe with us. If you need anything, all you have to do is ask."

I watch as he walks out, closing the door behind him. Then I scurry into the bathroom and close the door, dropping the blanket only once I'm utterly alone. I turn on the water until it's scalding hot. Even though it's the middle of summer, I'm frozen on the inside and my skin feels soiled from being groped by a man who had no right to touch me.

Sitting on the shower floor, I curl back into the ball I was behind the chair. Every time I close my eyes, I smell the stale cigarette stench of that chair, hear the horror film playing in the living room, and feel his body on top of mine.

Him.

I never heard his name. I never heard any of their names. So I guess I'll stick with the scary guy, frat boy, and woman in charge as I replay the last I don't know how many hours of my life.

Maybe that's the most disorienting thing about all of this? How long has it been since I woke up and dressed for my daily jog?

Was that this morning? Yesterday? Two days ago?

Time means nothing, although between my adrenaline fading and the hot water pounding my back, a weariness unlike anything I've ever felt takes hold. I lean my head against the shower wall and slide my legs forward, pressing my feet against the glass. The bruising on my thigh is dark and fresh, with none of the yellowing that comes with time. I suppose it wasn't that long ago, after all.

"I'm safe. I'm safe. I'm safe." I chant the words over and over as I grab the soap and take stock of my limbs, sliding the bar across my skin.

Tears fall down my cheeks without sound at the memory of my father calling me Lambchop. That was my mother's pet name for me, and I haven't heard it since she died. I need to call him and let him know I'm okay. He's probably worried sick, and although I don't want him to see me like this, I need to make sure he's okay, too.

Who will take care of him while I'm away?

Deep down, I know it's not my job. He's never relied on me. He's barely aware of where I am from one day to the next, but that doesn't mean I don't take care of him from the shadows.

There's a knock on the bathroom door. "Leti?"

I'm not sure whose voice that is, but I bring my knees up in an attempt to cover myself. "Yes?"

"Are you okay?"

The question makes me realize the water is barely lukewarm. I've been sitting here long enough to drain the water heater, lost in my mindless wandering far too long. "Yes. I'll be right out."

I quickly wash all my parts, making sure to get the soles of my feet, and then stand under the now cold spray, rinsing as quickly as possible. Turning off the water, I hear a noise on the other side of the door. "Hello?"

"It's me, Caiden. There are clothes for you on the bed. I'll be waiting for you in the living room. Okay?"

"Okay. I'll be out in a few minutes."

Once I hear the door close, I grab two towels—one for my hair and the other for my body—before I gently open the bathroom door and peek out into the bedroom. I'm not afraid of these men, but I've never been the type to walk around naked in front of strangers. Hell, I barely lounge around my own pool in a bikini without covering up. I always throw on something before going into the house where my father or any of the staff might see me.

That's one of many ways my sister and I differ. She's always been comfortable in her body and embraces her curves, while I've always hidden mine. It's not that I'm ashamed of my body, because I'm not, but I have never been comfortable with people looking at me.

On the bed are a pair of soft, well-worn gray sweatpants, a black ribbed tank top, a Townsend Security branded T-shirt, and an oversized Loyola sweatshirt. More layers than I need and yet, I'm thankful for them.

Dressed, I crack open the door and peer down the hallway, where I hear the men in the kitchen milling about as they fix a midnight snack.

"As soon as she comes out, before we sleep tonight, we need to see if we can get confirmation of Claudine's accomplices."

I'm not sure who is talking. They all have low, deep voices. Sexy and sensual, like the kinds of voices I'd love to have read me to sleep at night.

"That might be traumatic for her," another voice says.

"No choice," the gruffer of the three voices says, and I think that voice belongs to Reese. He seems to be the de facto leader of this group, although every one of them seems like they are in charge.

"Leti?" Caiden, the man who carried me out of that awful house, steps into view at the end of the hallway. He gives me a gentle smile and waves me forward with a tilt of his head. "Come have some tea or hot cocoa."

I walk toward him and follow him into the kitchen where Reese and Soren also stand around the island with a loaf of bread and an assortment of lunch meats, peanut butter and jelly.

Reese motions to the food. "How about a PB&J to help settle your stomach?"

"We're sure you haven't eaten in a long time," Caiden adds.

"How long?" I ask. "How long since they took me?"

Glancing from man to man, I realize how big each of them is. Soren is the smallest, but he's still a good five inches taller than me, with broad shoulders, a thick neck, and a dark, trim beard. His blue eyes are the most striking and the permanent blush reddening his cheeks gives him a boyish charm.

Reese is the biggest. At least six foot six with a massive chest that his T-shirt struggles to contain. He has the hardest face, the shrewdest, dark gaze, and a crooked nose with a small scar on his cheek that tells tales of past fights.

Caiden has a bit of a Calvin Klein underwear model to him, with high cheekbones and a five o'clock shadow darkening his cheeks. His eyes are hazel, or maybe gray. Honestly, it's hard to tell in this light, but he has dark thick eyelashes—the kind every girl goes gaga over.

They glance at each other and Reese says, "A little over eighteen hours."

"That's it?" It feels like a lifetime.

"It was eighteen hours longer than it should have been." Soren looks up from the tablet in his hands and pins me with his blue eyes.

"Come." Caiden gently guides me to a seat at a four-person dining table. "Let us make you a sandwich. Would you prefer tea or something else?"

"What time is it?"

"It's a little after midnight." He arches his brow as if he wants to ask me why and then decides against it.

"Do we have coffee?"

"Decaf?" Caiden and Reese exchange a look.

"No. Regular." I know I should, but I don't want to go to sleep. If closing my eyes for a couple seconds in the shower wreaked havoc on my subconscious, what is sleep going to do?

"Okay." Reese nods, sliding his hand down his face. "I'll make some coffee while Caiden makes you a sandwich. Meanwhile, you should call your sister and father and let them know you are safe."

I lower my eyes and nod, knowing he is right. "Okay."

ENTES TUERE
PUNIRE IMPIOS

COFFEE AT MIDNIGHT. If she was up and out for a run at six-thirty, she's most likely a morning person and not a night owl, which means she is avoiding sleep for obvious reasons. But having her mentally exhausted is not good for any of us.

If she was an uncooperative witness placed in our custody, I wouldn't be above slipping her some valerian root or some other gentle sleep aid, but the last thing I want to do is betray her trust. She's our client, yes, but there is something about her that calls to my primal need to protect her at all costs.

Everything about her profile says she's intelligent, with a good head on her shoulders. It also says she's lonely and sheltered, although I've yet to determine if that is self-imposed or a result of losing her mother at such a young age. She diverged from her sister's path at some point, and although her father does seem genuinely concerned about his daughters, his interaction with Epiphany left a lot to be desired.

What would his interaction with Leti be like and would I approve?

I put on a pot of coffee, regular, because we don't have decaf anyway, while Caiden puts a sandwich and a glass of water on the table in front of her.

Soren sets up his computer and slides a phone in front of her. "Who would you like to talk to first?"

"My sister, I guess." She picks a corner of the sandwich apart and pops the smallest morsel into her mouth.

"We'll give you some privacy," Caiden says, motioning to Soren to follow him into the living area. Caiden sits at one end of the couch, while Soren sits in the chair with his computer on his lap.

I pretend to be oblivious as she stares at the phone screen, not making a move to hit send.

I'm about to ask her what she wants in her coffee when she stands abruptly, taking the phone with her into the living room and sitting on the couch, practically in Caiden's lap. Their thighs are touching. His arm already stretched over the top of the sofa falls naturally behind her head as she settles back and hits the call button, the conversation on speaker.

"Yeah?" Lee answers just as gruffly as before. Considering I chewed his ass earlier when Epiphany answered the secure line, I'm guessing he's still pissed.

"Hey, man," Caiden says gently. "Leti's ready to talk to her sister."

Lee's tone softens. "I'll bring her the phone."

"Leti?" Epiphany's voice comes over the speaker.

"Hi, Pip." Leti has her head down, her chin low, her damp hair covering her face. Her words are upbeat, but the voice behind them doesn't sell positivity.

Caiden looks up with wide eyes, especially when she rests her hand on the seam where their bodies meet, her fingers brushing the outside of his thigh. I presume she's seeking comfort, like she did in the car with her toes under Soren's thigh, which only emphasizes how starved for physical touch she is. How many years has she survived hugging teddy bears instead of flesh and blood while living in the cold mansion on the hill?

There are many documented benefits to human touch. A hug is said to raise serotonin and decrease cortisol levels. Massage stimulates an increased release of healing oxytocin to the body. And sex... dear god, I shouldn't think about her and the documented benefits of sex in the same thought process.

She's our client.

Our beautiful client with a sweet, almost naïve charm —which is my catnip—but she's still a client, nonetheless.

I bring a mug of coffee over to the couch and place it on the table in front of her. She reaches out and grabs my hand with a forcefulness that surprises me, pulling me down to sit beside her. Now she's sandwiched between Caiden and me, the phone on speaker resting on her thigh, her palms flat on our legs.

Neither of us says a word as dead air plays between the twins.

"I'm sorry," Epiphany finally says.

"Why?" Leti shakes her head. We can't see her face. I can't see her eyes. But we feel the tension ratcheting through her limbs as she squeezes our thighs. As if we are also twins born of the same mind, both Caiden and I place a hand on top of hers, interlacing our fingers and resting our joined hands between our legs. This seems to calm her enough to get her talking. "You have nothing to be sorry about. I'm sorry for all the trouble this is causing you. I'm sure being hundreds of miles away is disrupting your business. Your fans miss you."

Soren watches us with interest, the computer in his lap holding none of his attention, as his eyes follow our innocent and yet meaningful coupling.

"Fuck them." Epiphany chokes back a sob, which seems to cause Leti more distress. "You're my sister. You are the only thing that matters. If anything had happened to you... well, they told me you're fine. Is that true?"

"Yes," Leti says, barely above a whisper.

Epiphany sniffles on the other end of the line. "Dammit. I told myself to hold it together and be strong for you and now I'm blubbering. I'm sorry."

Oh dammit. I wish these women would stop apologizing to each other and say what they really mean.

"Are you okay?" Leti whispers again, as if she's afraid of asking the question more than hearing the answer, which makes me wonder what kind of emotional abuse she's experienced over the years. Can such a simple question equate to backlash? If so, my feelings for Epiphany and her welfare are diminishing by the second.

"I'm fine. I was lounging by the pool, completely

oblivious, as usual, when our father called me. I don't even know how he got my number." Epi chuckles, but it doesn't hold an ounce of warmth.

"How is he?" Leti asks.

"He's worried, obviously, but he trusts the men he hired to protect us. And, well, I guess he was right. We are safe and secure."

I can't stop myself from squeezing Leti's hand.

For the first time, she lifts her chin and grants me a small smile.

Damn, what I wouldn't give to make her smile for real all the time. This woman needs some affection and kindness in her life. She needs to hear words of love and affirmation daily until she not only expects them, she demands them. She deserves to be adored, worshipped, and treated like the queen she's meant to be—and fuck, why is my mind going to places it's not supposed to go?

Leti has the soft shell over a hardened demeanor that attracts men like me. I want to protect her while peeling those layers away until I get to the squishy, gooey, warm center of her heart—one she is desperate to give, but too jaded after years of mistreatment to share.

"Leti, when this is over—" Epiphany pauses and clears her throat "—can we hang out? I know I've been a horrible sister, just like Walter told me he's been a horrible father to us. While I can't do anything about him, I'd like to make some changes and get to know my twin."

I can feel the fear in Leti build as she tamps down the elation threatening to burst from her throat. She wants nothing more than a close connection with her sister, but she's terrified, too.

Leti replies in an even, monotone voice, her small palm sweating in my huge hand. "Of course we can hang out. Whatever your schedule allows, Pip, I'll make myself available."

"The only thing on my schedule is hanging out with my sister. I know you don't believe me because I've fucked you so many times in the past, but I'm going to prove it to you, Leti. We can hang out at the house or go on a vacation somewhere—whatever you want—but it will be you and me. No cameras. No live casts. No Instagram pictures. Just me and my sister."

Leti giggles, her hand relaxing in mine. "Okay. I believe you."

"I can't wait to hug you again," Epiphany says, her voice growing small on the line.

Without a word, Leti drops my hand and jumps to her feet, taking the phone with her as she runs down the hall into her bedroom. The door closes, and we're left with an uncomfortable silence filled with *what the fuck happened* written all over our faces.

Caiden exhales a breath that I'm betting he's been holding for the past several minutes. "We're in trouble."

Soren nods, but says nothing.

I rub my eyes and pinch the bridge of my nose. "It's not possible."

"When has anything ever come easy to us?" Caiden rubs his hands on his thighs and stands, grabbing the untouched cup of coffee and walking back into the kitchen.

"She's an innocent. Not to mention, our brutalized client."

"Who better than us to take care of her?" Caiden places his palms on the edge of the counter and looks at me, his voice just loud enough to reach our ears.

Shaking my head, I have every intention of shooting him down, but instead I can't stop the words as they leave my lips. "No one."

ENTES TUERE
PUNIRE IMPIOS

JEALOUSY PUMPS THROUGH MY VEINS—ITS tangy bitterness bubbling up and touching the back of my tongue, leaving a rancid taste in my mouth. When Leti slid her toes underneath my thigh in the car, I froze—positive I should not call attention to the intimate, if also innocuous, touch. But when she started crying, I couldn't stop myself from reaching out and rubbing her exposed calf. Considering she calmed down instantly, I'm confident it was the right move.

But watching my partners surround her in a Leti sandwich fills me with a sense of possessiveness I've yet experienced when the three of us have bedded a woman. There's something about our brains that makes taking a woman together feel natural. From the first time it happened, we knew this is the way it will always be for us. At first it was fun, especially for me, who is by far the least experienced of the three of us. I was a virgin when I entered the military and only lost it on a drunken night during our first break from training. But after we got out of the military and settled in Chicago, we talked about wanting more.

We talked about finding the one who would complete our family.

Obviously, finding a woman who will take on a relationship with three men isn't easy. Finding a woman all three of us are attracted to? Just as difficult. But Caiden summed up all of our feelings in three simple words: *We're in trouble.*

She's the one. No doubt in my mind. In Caiden's mind. Or Reese's.

But he's right. Now is not the time. We are on a mission. She was brutalized, if not physically, definitely mentally. And while she seems perfectly attuned to our style of soft dominance, the question we have to ask and answer is when?

The door to the bedroom cracks open, and Leti comes down the hallway with a throw blanket and pillow. She presses her lips together, her eyes bouncing from Caiden in the kitchen to Reese on the couch and then to me. "I'm sorry about that."

Reese shakes his head and takes the phone she offers. "It's fine. Do you want to talk to your father?"

"Do you think we can put that off until tomorrow?" She tries for a smile, but it doesn't quite land.

"I'll text Victor and let him know you went to bed."

"You should try to get some sleep, Leti." Caiden says from the kitchen.

"Do you think we could watch a movie or something?" She twirls her finger over her head. "I need a distraction to quiet my mind and I don't have any of my usual tools."

I stand and set my laptop down on the coffee table. "What would you like to watch?"

"Whatever you want to watch will be fine." Leti sits in the middle of the couch, placing the pillow and blanket on her lap.

Kneeling in front of her, I place my hand on her knee and shake my head. "No, Leti. You tell me what you want, and I'll make it happen."

She brings her jade green eyes up to meet mine. "I'd like to watch one of the Scooby-Doo movies."

I chuckle. "Really?"

She smiles and nods, a light blush hitting her cheeks. "They're my favorite. I always watch them when I'm sad or sick."

Damn, her smile could light up a room. It definitely does something funny to my insides. Now it's my mission to make her smile as often as possible. "Get comfortable and I'll have it on in a few minutes."

Reese motions to me and then turns to Leti as she scoots closer to him. "There's one thing we need to do before we start watching a movie."

"Okay." She curls her legs underneath her, her knee resting on his thigh. "What?"

He looks down and then back at her, letting out a slow breath. "We need you to look at a few pictures and let us know if you recognize any of the people."

She stiffens, her gaze bouncing between us, her voice utterly defeated. "Oh. Okay."

I open the lid to my computer and swing it around to face her. The first picture that comes to life is of Claudine Humphreys.

She sucks in her breath. "Who is she?"

"Your sister's ex-IT manager. I guess she came to Epiphany with a business proposal that your sister passed on, and now Claudine has a grudge she thinks is worth near one hundred and fifty million dollars."

"One hundred and fifty?" Leti's eyes pop wide. "Wow."

"Are you giving us a positive ID?" Reese asks.

"Yes, that's definitely her."

"Okay." I take a deep breath because the last thing I want to do is upset her. "We are going to flip through some potential associates, and you let us know if any of them are familiar."

She unconsciously curls into herself again, bringing her knees up, squeezing the pillow against her chest. "Okay."

Earlier, I performed a search and scoured the internet, both public and private databases, for Claudine and any online communications she might have had in the last six months. I found a couple of encrypted conversations I have yet to crack, but I was able to trace them back to the non-secure IP address of the recipient. Then I cross-checked them with the computer's physical location and its MAC address, and I'm ninety percent sure I found the right guy. After I pulled up his arrest record—

aggravated assault, attempted rape, battery and false imprisonment—I'm even more confident.

He is a big guy and the idea of him manhandling Leti sets my blood to boil. I've yet to share this winner's details with Reese and Caiden. The laundry list of charges will send Reese through the roof and Caiden into the corner to clean his guns. He's already talked about putting a bullet between the guy's eyes once. His rap sheet will solidify Caiden's feelings on the matter.

I advance the screen and bring up contestant number one: Joe P. Dawson.

Leti lowers her chin and nods. "That's him."

I make eye contact with Reese and shake my head, letting him know without speaking a word how bad this guy is. The way his jaw tightens tells me he understands.

"This is the one who assaulted you?" I say gently.

"Yes, but there was another guy, too. Although he never touched me."

"Another guy?" Reese says with a forced casualness to his voice.

"Yeah. He spoke about Pip, so he might know her."

"What did he look like?" I ask.

She frowns. "Like a frat boy. That's what I called him in my head. He was tall and thin in comparison to that guy. Clean cut with sandy brown hair."

"What was his role?"

Leti shakes her head. "I don't know. Maybe he was the driver? This guy tackled me to the ground and then tied me up in the back of an old tan van. Claudine was sitting in the passenger seat. I never saw the driver's face, only his profile. I only saw him when he brought in a box of food and water before they left."

I flip through a couple more pictures, but none of them is the man she described. All of these guys have criminal records, so I obviously need to broaden my search. "Okay. That's it for tonight." I close my laptop and turn it away from her.

"Anything in particular you can tell us about the van?" Caiden asks, as he places her sandwich on the table.

She shrugs. "Old, weathered, tan. It stuck out in our neighborhood, but I figured they were workmen looking for an address."

"Okay. That's it for now." Reese pats her knee. "Do you want to lie down?"

"Maybe later. I think I'll eat that sandwich now," Leti says, putting the pillow aside.

"Okay." He moves to stand, and she squeaks in a panicked voice. "Where are you going?"

"Caiden and I need to call the other team and make sure they know what we know. Meanwhile, Soren is going to get your movie started and stay with you." He smiles at her. "We'll be back before the opening credits are over."

I take my tablet and connect it to the television, planning to retake my seat in the armchair when Leti pats the cushion Caiden previously occupied. "Sit with me, please."

"Only if you finish your sandwich." I flash her a teasing grin.

She takes a big bite, chewing thoughtfully as she leans back on the cushions.

Plopping down beside her, I mutter without thinking, "Good girl."

Sucking in her breath, Leti leans her body against mine, molding herself to me like a second skin. She practically purrs as she nestles close to me.

I swallow the lump building in my throat and croak out, "Are you ready to start the movie?"

"Yes, please."

ENTES TUERE
PUNIRE IMPIOS

"CONFIRMATION ON THE TAN VAN, Claudine, and this douchebag, Joe P. Dawson. We're sending you a photo now."

"Fucking tan van," Lee hisses at the same time that Case grumbles, "He looks like a douchebag."

"He hurt her," I say so low, I'm not sure they hear me. "If you get the chance before I do, you make him suffer."

"Roger," Case responds on autopilot.

"I'm serious, Case," I growl, rage bubbling up from under the surface. "Bare minimum, I want a bullet between his eyes, but I'd prefer to cut on him first."

They meet my comment with silence, but then Lee sighs. "We hear you."

"I guess we're on lock down until they either find us or Victor finds them," Case says.

"Yeah. Call if you learn anything." Reese stares at me as he speaks.

"Same." Lee hangs up on us.

I rub my head, frustration taking over. Me and idle don't mix. Sitting in place waiting for them to find us or find the other team goes against our training. And while Victor is the best—he did train us, after all—I don't like the idea of waiting for him to find this bitch and give us the all clear either.

Plus, I really want a shot at Dawson.

"You need to relax," Reese says as I pace back and forth in front of the Suburban. We went out to the garage to make sure Leti couldn't overhear any part of our conversation. "Your tension is triggering, and we're trying to get her to sleep."

"And to stop touching us." I hang my head and take in the garage floor.

"Are we really trying to get her to stop touching us?" Reese points out.

"We've met war prisoners less starved for physical touch. What the fuck is wrong with her family?"

He shakes his head. "I don't know, but it makes me wonder what a couple hours with Epiphany have been like for the Alpha-3 team?"

"Pure fucking torture." I chuckle, remembering Epiphany's bratty outburst in the library.

"A different kind of torture. We're in our own personal hell with Leti. She craves touch, but not the kind we want to give her. Besides, it would be inappropriate."

"Do you think she's..." I chew on the inside of my cheek, debating if I should voice aloud the question that's been bouncing around in my head.

"Seems like it."

"Fuck." I groan, turning my back to him. "Twenty-two and untouched. That's a damn shame."

"Even if she's not, she's still too innocent for the likes of us."

"We're gentle for three badass motherfuckers." I flash him a teasing smile. I mean, I know he's right, but I hate being shot down so easily.

He rolls his eyes. "She's going to keep touching us—reaching out and seeking comfort—and we're not going to be able to deny her."

"Then we don't. We won't initiate contact, but we won't shy away either." I shrug. "It seems pretty easy to me."

"Yeah, until your balls turn blue after being perpetually turned on for days on end. We don't know how long this mission is going to last."

I shrug. "I can jack off in the shower. It's no different from every other night."

He shakes his head. "There is something wrong with you."

"You think?"

Reese rolls his eyes. "Let's get in there. I told her we wouldn't miss the opening credits."

When we enter the house, we find Soren sitting on one end of the couch, but it's not until we come around to face him that we find Leti's head resting on a pillow in his lap.

He shakes his head, his cheeks flushed red. "She wouldn't sleep any other way."

I shrug. "We give her whatever she needs."

She opens her eyes and grants me a small smile, pushing herself to sit up. "You're back. Come sit on the couch with us and watch the movie."

I sit on the other end of the couch while she watches my every move, and return her smile. "Eyes on the screen, Leti."

Moving the pillow from Soren's lap to mine, she lies her head down and brings her legs up on the couch. With silent movement, Soren adjusts the blanket and settles her feet in his lap, his hand resting on her calf.

Reese slumps down in the chair next to us, kicking his feet up on the coffee table. We are bone tired, the day's events finally catching up to us. Absent-mindedly, I stroke her hair, lean my head back, and close my eyes. During our training we learned how to sleep sitting up, propped against a tree, with our eyes open. This is damn comfortable in comparison. It takes nothing for me to fall asleep.

I'M NOT sure how long we're out, but my head snaps up and my adrenaline pumps when Leti whimpers and then screams, kicking her legs and flailing her hands. I pull her into my arms, cradling her against my chest. "It's okay, baby girl. We're here. You're safe."

She clutches at my chest, burying her face into my neck. Worming her way onto my lap, she straddles my thighs and clings to me in a way that both fills and breaks my heart at the same time.

"Shhh." I close my eyes, shutting out the room as she sinks into me. I've never felt such warmth and a need for love radiating off another person. I'm sure she doesn't love me—how could she when she doesn't know me—but this is what it feels like when someone trusts you. Maybe this is the result of the trauma she experienced, or maybe she's so desperate for someone to trust, someone to care for her, someone to love—and instinctively she knows it's us.

Either way, I'm going to soak it up while I can.

I feel Reese and Soren staring at us. I'm sure they are jealous. I would be too, if I weren't the one holding her in my arms. Standing, I make quick eye contact with them and then carry her down the hall into the primary bedroom. She wraps her legs around me like she's afraid I'll let go.

She doesn't understand. I'm never letting go.

"Baby. You're safe."

Shaking her head, her breath is hot on my neck and the press of her body against mine speaks to my most basic needs as a man. I need to protect her, covet her, own her mind, body, and spirit.

"Come on now," I say gently as I sit on the edge of the bed with her in my lap. "Be a good girl and show me your eyes."

She tenses with my words, her fingers curling into fists at my back, her ankles hooked around my waist. Bringing her head up, her jade green eyes flash as they lock with mine. "I'm sorry."

I smile, smoothing back a strand of her hair. "Nothing to be sorry about."

"I don't mean to be so much trouble." She bites her lip without wincing, bringing my eyes down to her mouth. Despite the cut, they are pink and plump and give me so many ideas.

"You're not any trouble. We're here to protect you, and if we can provide comfort, we're here for that, too."

Her eyes close, and without warning, she presses her lips against mine.

I freeze, fully aware of the precipice we're balanced precariously on at this moment. I want to respond. I want to roll her to her back, slip my tongue between her lips and claim her in the first of many ways. But I also know that once I start, I'm not going to want to stop.

Instead, I grip her shoulders and pull her back. "What are you doing, Leti?"

She shakes her head, a red blush hitting her cheeks. "I'm sorry."

Sighing, I run my hands up her neck and slide my thumb softly across her cheeks. "Baby, you never have to apologize to me. But you've had a traumatic experience, and I don't want your emotions causing you to do something you'll regret later."

"I want to feel something," she whispers.

I press my forehead to hers and whisper, "If this was any other time, any other place, I would want to make you feel those things."

"You would?"

"More than I could say right now. If you want to have that conversation after you've had a good night's sleep, you can ask me later. For now, I need you to go to bed."

"Are you going to leave me?" She whimpers.

"Nope. I'm going to lie right beside you, and either Reese or Soren will lie on the other side of you. We're here anytime you need to reach out for us, and we'll continue to be here until you don't need us anymore."

"Can we all sleep on the bed?"

I glance over her shoulder at my partners standing in the doorway. She takes my cue and turns to look behind her back. A small squeak comes out as a deep blush darkens her cheeks.

Reese shakes his head. "The bed's not big enough for four of us, doll, but we're right outside the door."

ENTES TUERE
PUNIRE IMPIOS

Chapter Nine

I WAKE UP ALONE, but hear their voices outside the room, and smell coffee and bacon and something sweet like cinnamon rolls.

"You're awake." Caiden comes into the bedroom carrying a mug.

Yawning, I stretch my arms over my head. "Wow. I really zonked out."

"You needed to sleep. How do you feel?" He sits on the edge of the bed out of reach.

I glance at the space between us. It feels like a mile, although it's only a couple of inches. Is he distancing himself after the way I acted last night? I know female emotions make most men uncomfortable. They certainly make my father uneasy.

My fingers twitch as I tamp down a desperate need to reach out to him. "Silly. I'm so sorry for the way I carried on last night."

He smiles and fingers a lock of my hair, demonstrating how close we really are right now. "We have a new rule in this house."

"What's that?"

"You are no longer allowed to say I'm sorry." He winks and lightly taps the tip of my nose.

"I'm—"

He raises his brow, effectively cutting me off.

Blushing, I press my lips together, swallowing the forbidden word.

"Good girl." Smiling, he stands and takes a sip from his mug. "Are you hungry?"

"I am."

"Good. Reese and I have been cooking all morning, but we are waiting for you. Why don't you do what you need to do in the bathroom and then come meet us in the kitchen so we can start our day?"

He leaves, almost closing the door behind him, but leaving it open a crack to show he's not locked out and I'm not locked in. I find it odd how every movement these men make seems to be deliberate, as if they design every action with my feelings in mind.

Rushing into the bathroom, I make quick work with the toothbrush and toothpaste, a washcloth and some facial soap. I brush the tangles out of my hair and pull it into a ponytail, using a soft scrunchie I find on the counter. I don't remember the facial cleanser or the hair products being there last night, but I was in such a state, maybe I missed them?

It's warm this morning, so I pull off the sweatshirt, leaving me in their soft cotton T-shirt and walk down the hallway to meet them in the kitchen. Caiden is sitting at the table with his coffee while Reese leans against the corner of the counter with his arms crossed over his broad chest. Soren sits in the living room with his computer on his lap.

"Good morning." Reese uncrosses his arms and beckons me to him with a crook of his finger. He went from closed off and formidable to welcoming with that one motion, and I can't stop my feet as I run into his open arms. He engulfs me with his long muscled limbs, his chest hard and yet soothing. I melt against him, feeling loving warmth radiate off of his skin.

Maybe I'm imagining it.

Maybe I am making something out of nothing, turning years of fairytales and fantasies into a false reality, but I don't care.

At this moment, happiness runs through my veins.

"How did you sleep, doll?" Reese's words rumble through his chest, making me not only hear, but feel him.

"Good. What time is it?"

"It's almost one."

I lift my head. "One in the afternoon? Oh my gosh, I had no idea I slept so long. I apologize for my outburst last night."

Behind us, Caiden clears his throat. "What did you say?"

Blushing, I turn to look at him. "You said I couldn't say the S word."

Caiden shakes his head, his lips curled slightly at the

corners as he exchanges a look with Reese. "Our girl thinks she's clever."

Reese hooks his finger underneath my chin and turns my head to face him. "Now, doll, I know for a fact Caiden told you that you're no longer allowed to say *I'm sorry* in this house, and that includes all words that effectively mean the same thing. You never have to apologize to us for being emotional, vulnerable, or needy. We want you to need us. We want to comfort you. We're here to protect you for as long as you need and want us to."

I hear what he's saying. I even understand what he is saying, but I'm having a hard time comprehending and believing it. I've spent my life staying out of people's way, prepared for them to be angry when I am too clingy. So he surely can't mean what he is saying right now. He doesn't want me to share my feelings with him. No one ever does, but I appreciate the sentiment. To pacify him, I smile and nod. "Okay."

Reese leans down and puts his mouth near my ear. I lean into his body and shiver when his warm breath hits my skin. "Soren has had that damn computer on his lap all morning. I think he needs a break. Maybe you should ask him for a hug?"

I look up to find Reese smiling down at me. "Do you think?"

"Yeah. If you ask him for a hug, I'm positive he'll put that computer down and come eat brunch with us."

I grin, feeling light as a butterfly. Not only am I being given permission to initiate physical contact, I'm encouraged to. "Okay."

Without thinking, I lift on my tiptoes and press a kiss to Reese's cheek before dancing across the room to stop beside Soren's chair. His head snaps up, as if he didn't realize I was in the room. "Good morning, Leti."

"Good morning." I squat next to him and lean my chin on the armrest, looking up at him through my lashes. "Can I have a hug?"

He narrows his eyes and then looks over at the kitchen before bringing his eyes back to me. His blue eyes morph from cold to dazzling. "You want a hug from me?"

I nod. "Please."

His movements are smooth as he moves the computer off his lap and stands, pulling me to my feet. He wraps his arms around me and rests his chin on the top of my head. I melt a little. The amount of love and kindness they have shown me since waking up is over-whelming.

He chuckles. "You give amazing hugs."

"Really?" I squeeze him tighter.

"Yeah. I could stand here holding you forever." He places a kiss against my temple. "But the murderous looks I'm getting from my partners say it's time to eat."

I giggle and let him go. "I'm hungry, too."

After we get settled in our seats, the guys dig into their plates. After a few minutes of silent eating, Reese wipes his mouth with a napkin. "What's a normal weekend look like for you, Leti?"

"What do you mean?" I say around a mouth full of pancakes.

"What do you do when you aren't working and not

cooped up with a bunch of smelly guys in a safe house in the middle of Peoria?"

I giggle. "You guys aren't smelly."

"Not yet," Soren points out. "Just wait until these two work out."

"Shut up, ass." Caiden chuckles and elbows Soren, who is sitting to his right.

I like the way they interact with each other. Kind of like brothers, but there is something more. While I feel protected by them, I feel like they'd also die to protect each other, too. They have a real family vibe to them that goes beyond working together.

"Well, I get up at six every morning, go for a run, then take a shower. On Saturdays I make myself an omelet, but on Sundays I bake something new."

"You like to bake?" Caiden raises his brow.

"Yeah," I duck my head. "I like to try new recipes. My mother was an excellent baker."

"That's nice. You keep her memory alive with your pastries," Reese says, reaching out and rubbing my knee under the table.

"I could pick you up a list of ingredients today, if you want to bake while we are here," Soren says.

I lift my head. "Really?"

"Yeah. We love to eat." He nods.

"We'll eat anything you feed us," Caiden chuckles.

Reese removes his hand from my leg and crumbles a napkin, throwing it across the table to land on Caiden's plate. "Ass."

"What did he say?" I look between them. Reese's eyes narrowed on Caiden, who wears a wide, goofy grin.

"Ignore them, Leti. Sometimes they are no better than a couple of teenage boys who have stumbled upon their first Playboy magazine." Soren rolls his eyes.

I know I'm naïve for my age. My experience level is almost zero, even though I'm not a virgin. I dated the same guy—my only boyfriend—for two and a half years while in college. Matt went to Northwestern University and was a brother from Sigma Alpha Epsilon. We met at a charity event that my sorority and his fraternity co-sponsored. While he never made my heart flutter, on paper we were the perfect overachieving couple—like his parents.

Both attending excellent schools.

Both from wealthy families.

Both with what others consider "good pedigrees".

Under pressure from my sorority sisters, I started dating Matt my sophomore year. He didn't demand a lot of my time, and we spent most of our dates at the library. Occasionally, he'd take me to dinner, which was usually at his parent's house. They were as stiff and cold as my father, a loveless marriage born of the same fodder that brought me and Matt together. Even though Matt proposed my senior year and I said yes, my heart wasn't in it. I did it more out of obligation, thinking it would make my father happy.

It didn't.

Although I gave Matt my virginity—deep down, I did it because I hoped sex would bring us closer. Unfortunately, sex with him was passionless and boring. It brought about none of the feelings I've read about in books, and it didn't seem like he wanted to do it with me anymore than I wanted to do it with him. Over the last four months of our relationship, we had sex a handful of times and then, right before we graduated, I found out why.

Matt, while quiet and reserved with me, was a renown freak with a handful of girls at his college. His brothers called him Mad Matt, and he bedded two or more girls at every frat party, usually at the same time. Everyone knew, but nobody felt the need to tell me. I had no idea what he was doing, leaving me completely humiliated once I found out.

Needless to say, I broke off the engagement. He wasn't happy, because he thought he could replicate his parents' picture-perfect marriage for high society, while having his dirty little secrets that weren't really secrets at all—like his father.

Like I said, I know I'm naïve, but I'm not stupid. There's a loose level of tension between the men at the kitchen table right now, and something tells me it's about me.

Do they know I tried to kiss Caiden last night? Are they mad? They don't seem to be mad at me at all. I've never had so much welcomed contact from one person, much less three.

Thinking of that lame kiss last night. I'd really like to try it again. A do-over, if I could. I don't have a lot of experience, and I'm sure I need to practice. What if I'm a terrible kisser, and that's the reason Matt never tried to be with me like he was with the others?

If Epiphany and I were closer, we could talk about these things. I've seen pictures of her kissing on the red carpet, as well as at different celebrity parties. My sister is probably an excellent kisser, not that she and I have ever talked about anything like that. She's far too busy to have conversations like that with me.

"Back to the ingredients," Soren says, at the same time as I ask, "Do you look at Playboy often?"

Caiden chuckles while Reese swears under his breath. "No, doll. Looking at pictures of naked women doesn't really do it for us."

"What does?" My eyes are on what's left of my pancake, but I can feel the collective sucking in of breath around the table. I'm probably overstepping my boundaries—I know I am—but for some reason, I really want to know what makes them tick.

What gets them excited?

What kind of woman turns each of them on?

I dare to bring my eyes up, finding each of them staring back at me. *I'm sorry* is on the tip of my tongue, but I swallow it down.

"There's a good possibility we're going to be together for a couple of days. Are you sure you want to have this kind of conversation with us?"

"I didn't mean to make you uncomfortable."

Caiden smiles. "You couldn't make us uncomfortable if you tried, but we don't want you to be embarrassed around us, ever."

ENTES TUERE
PUNIRE IMPIOS

Chapter Ten

REESE

I'M GOING to kill Caiden, but am I really any better? After watching Leti cling to him last night and then knowing she kissed him in the bedroom, I felt a primal need to open myself up and let her seek comfort from me this morning. And then, after I felt her melt against me, I sent her to Soren, manipulating her into seeking warmth and affection from all three of us.

I have no doubt she wants what we have to offer her— at least part of it. Taking that next step, wanting us to take her as a man takes a woman, is the furthest thing from her mind.

Wanting three men to take her the way we want to has probably never even been a fantasy.

Although, she did ask what turns us on. Do we tell her and risk her hiding from us until this is over?

Fuck me, I know the answer. The answer is we keep this professional and keep our hands to ourselves.

But damned if that's what I'm going to do.

"I'm not embarrassed." She bites her lip, and it does things to me. She's sexy in the most demure and unobvious way. I doubt she understands how much something as simple as biting her lip turns me on.

"The three of us have been together a long time, doll. We met when we were seventeen and nineteen years old. We've gone through training, been in combat, and currently live and work together. We do everything together."

Caiden adds in, "He means everything."

The three of us sit perfectly still as her gaze bounces from her plate to each of us and back again. There's a deep blush hitting her cheeks, but to her credit, she doesn't back down. "I've never heard of such a thing. I've heard of one man with multiple women. My ex does that."

Soren's eyes pop wide. "With you?"

She shakes her head. "No. He did it behind my back."

"One thing you need to know about us, doll. We don't lie. Ever."

"Hmmm," Leti murmurs, playing with the napkin in her lap. "I've never heard of such a thing."

We sit in silence for several minutes, letting her process this information. She doesn't make eye contact with us, but she doesn't run away.

I suppose I should call this a win?

Soren fidgets in his seat before jumping up to clear his and Caiden's plate. Then he walks over to her side, crouching beside her. "We are still the same men who pulled you out of that wretched house yesterday. Still the same men who watched Scooby Doo with you last night. You promised you wouldn't be uncomfortable with us."

She looks at him and, I think, smiles. "I'm not embarrassed. I'm trying to imagine how that would work."

Caiden laughs. "Don't think too hard, baby."

I glare at him. "Shut up."

Soren rolls his eyes. "If I pick up the ingredients, will you bake for us?"

She cups his cheek. "Yes."

"What else do you do when you aren't working?" I prompt.

Shrugging, she finally looks me and Caiden in the eye. "I read. Listen to music. Attend yoga in the afternoon. Then there is dinner, followed by a movie, and then back to bed with a book."

Such a regiment, and it sounds lonely. I don't say this out loud, but I see the look that passes over Caiden's face that confirms he shares my thoughts.

AN HOUR LATER, both Caiden and Soren have left for the store, leaving Leti and me alone. She begrudgingly gave Soren a list of beauty products she uses, protesting she doesn't want to be any trouble. She's still bitching about it as I finish washing the dishes.

"You don't have to do special stuff for me." She

throws down the dish towel. "I don't want to be any trouble."

I grab her upper arm and swing her around so she bounces against my chest. Then I back her against the counter and tilt her chin up so that she has no choice but to look me in the eye. "You're no trouble to us, doll. We want to take care of and pamper you. It is our pleasure to do so. Okay?"

She blinks rapidly, pressing her lips together. "Okay."

Staring down at her, her jade green eyes sparkle. "I wish we'd met under different circumstances."

"Really? You would have talked to me if we'd met at the gym?"

"Probably not." I frown. "I don't make eye contact with women at the gym. I'm very focused on my workout. But anywhere else—absolutely."

"No one like you has ever paid attention to me."

"Men are stupid." I grin.

"I've only had one boyfriend, and he only wanted me to satisfy some high society checklist. Dutiful wife from a pedigreed family with the right amount of class, education, and money. I've never flirted or been flirted with. I wouldn't have known how to respond if we'd met under different circumstances." She bites the right side of her lip again.

"There are all kinds of flirting to be done. Some are overt. Some are subtle." I smooth my thumb over her bottom lip, freeing it from her teeth. "Like every time you bite your lip, it sends blood rushing to my cock."

She sucks in her breath, her eyes wide.

"Does that offend you?" I don't back down, even though I know I should.

Shaking her head, she keeps her gaze locked with mine while her cheeks burn red. "No one talks to me that way."

"I shouldn't talk to you this way, but I can't help myself."

"I don't want you to stop." She clutches at my shirt.

"I really want to taste your lips and see if you are nearly as sweet as you look."

She drops her eyes. "I'm afraid I'm a horrible kisser."

Leaning down, I hover my mouth over hers and wait until she brings her eyes up to mine. "I'll be the judge of that."

I start slowly, brushing my lips over hers, knowing I'm destined for hell or the unemployment line—whichever comes first. Victor's going to kill me, but I don't think my partners will mind a little time off if it means we get her. Maybe we'll start our own company like the Delta-3 team did in New York. Darian, Xander, and Garrett have done well for themselves despite turning Victor down. From what I hear, they are happy with a little wife of their own.

Leti sighs, giving me unspoken permission to deepen the kiss. I lick the seam of her mouth and then plunge my tongue in when she opens for me. Sweetened with a hint of pancake syrup—I have no doubt she'd be delicious no matter what. Her tongue is tentative, as if she's unsure what to do, but her inexperience doesn't bother me in the least. If anything, it's a turn on. I wouldn't consider myself to be a Daddy Dom, but I definitely have some of the tendencies. I want to take care of her, teach and guide her. I'm not looking for a little girl, but I'm not turned off by her naïveté, either.

I run my hands down her sides and slide them under her ass, lifting and setting her on the counter. "Wrap your legs around me."

She does as she's told, and I flash her a smile. "Good girl."

"More," Leti whimpers.

"Mmmm," I growl, pulling her ponytail loose and threading my hands through her hair. "So demanding."

I kiss her until she's breathless. Until she's lost her inhibitions and kisses me back with the same fervor I have burning low in my belly. She clutches at my shirt as she locks her ankles behind my back, pulling me in tight against her body. I can feel her heat against my cock through my cargo pants, and it takes everything within me to pull back.

The guys are going to be pissed that I started without them, but I think this is what she needs. She needs us, but getting us at the same time would be overwhelming for somebody with her lack of experience. This is better. First a taste of me, then some time alone with Soren. She's already comfortable with Caiden, but he didn't get to taste her like I am right now.

I should feel bad for manipulating her like this, but it's for her own good. If I benefit from it, too, so be it.

First, we make her comfortable initiating physical contact with something as innocuous as a hug.

Then, she finds kissing us in private acceptable.

Then, it's easy to kiss us in front of each other.

And then? Jesus, I can't think about what comes after that.

"I think you're an excellent kisser, Leti. Caiden and Soren are going to think so, too."

Her green eyes sparkle. "They want to kiss me, too?"

"Oh, yeah."

"Isn't that wrong?"

I pull back to make sure she sees my face. "It's not conventional, but is it wrong to love who you love?"

"But, one woman with three men... what will people think?"

"Who gives a fuck?" I say with a bit more bark than I should. "What happens in our bedroom is nobody's goddamn business."

She unhooks her ankles and drops her legs from my waist. "I don't know."

Fuck! Me and my stupid fucking mouth. Sometimes I'm no better than a goddamn bull in a china shop.

I've pushed her too far, and now she is retreating, drawing back into herself. I slide my hand down my face, ready to kick my own ass for my stupidity. "I'm not asking you to make any life-changing decisions tonight, doll. I'm just saying don't dismiss what you're feeling because of societal norms."

"I've spent my entire life worrying about what other people think and feel," she says softly.

"And where has that gotten you?" I brush my thumb along her unbruised cheek. "Utterly alone with no one giving you an ounce of the attention, affection, or love you deserve."

Her brow furrows and her smile falls, and I know my bluntness has killed the mood.

She pushes me back and hops off the counter. "Excuse me for a minute," she whispers as she scurries down the hallway, shutting the bedroom door closed behind her.

Fuck me!

ENTES TUERE
PUNIRE IMPIOS

Chapter Eleven

OH MY GOD, what am I doing? I kissed Reese, or he kissed me—either way, we definitely made out and then...

My whole body is a tingly mess. I feel things I've only felt while reading a steamy romance in bed with my bedroom door locked. And when Reese said I should do the same thing with Soren and Caiden? Oh my god! Could I do something like that? Could I be with three different men at different times? Do they do this kind of stuff at the same time?

Yes, I suppose they do.

Back to wondering how that would work?

I hide in the bedroom long enough for Caiden and Soren to come home, and then for Soren to come knocking at my door. "Leti? Can I come in?"

I pull my knees into my chest. "Yes."

He walks in with two shopping bags and closes the door behind him. "Are you okay?"

"Did he tell you?" My embarrassment reddens my cheeks.

"I didn't wait to hear the story. Instead, I came to show you what I bought." He dumps the contents of the bags on the bed. "Shampoo, conditioner, body wash, and lotion. I guessed on your size and picked up a couple of T-shirts, shorts, and—" he blushes "—undergarments. Sorry to be presumptuous, but I thought you'd like to wear some clothes designed for women."

I finger through the fabrics, noting the lacy panties. They are feminine, beautiful, and unlike anything I've ever worn. I've never had a man who cared about undressing me, much less what I was wearing underneath my clothes. Do they expect me to wear this for them? I'm both nervous and excited by the idea. "This is very thoughtful of you."

"We want to make you as comfortable as possible while you are stuck here with us." He sits on the edge of the bed and stares at the floor. "Did Reese say something stupid while we were gone?"

"No. He didn't. But I'm afraid I'm not strong enough to be the kind of woman you want."

He brings his bright blue eyes up to meet mine. "You are the strongest woman I've ever met. Strong and beautiful—a true survivor."

"I'm socially awkward and alone." I hang my head, my own twisted version of Reese's words flying out of my mouth.

Soren lifts my chin so I have no choice but to look at him. "I'm awkward, and I used to be alone. There's nothing wrong with that, if that's what you want. But if you want more..."

He lets the words sit out there unspoken, but he doesn't have to complete the sentence to let me know what he means. I don't have to be alone. There are three men who want me, even though I have no idea why. We just met. They found me naked, dirty, and damn near catatonic. If they had rescued and immediately taken me home, I would be sitting in my room alone and breaking into sporadic crying fits, unable to sleep without being heavily medicated.

Instead, I'm safe and warm and feeling things I never thought I'd know as a woman. I'd resigned myself to being an old maid by the time I was thirty. A spinster shunned by society as if we lived during the Victorian era, destined to live in her father's big house while her twin sister travels the world falling in love with someone new every six months.

I roll onto my knees and lean forward, bringing my face within inches of Soren's. "I kissed Reese."

He nods but doesn't make a move toward me.

"And I kind of kissed Caiden last night."

"I know," he says softly.

I swallow the lump in my throat. "Reese said I should kiss you, too."

"Did he?" Soren leans forward, brushing his lips over mine. "What do you think about that?"

"I'm not sure what to think."

"Do you think we would do anything to hurt you?"

"No." I smile. "I know you wouldn't."

"Then what's there to think about?" Soren surprises me with a forceful kiss, pulling me on top of him as he lays back on the bed. His kiss is just as dominating and as skilled as Reese's, and yet being on top of him gives me a sense of power and control I didn't feel earlier. I place my knees on either side of his hips, moaning as he plunges his tongue inside my mouth. His hands are everywhere, cradling my neck before sliding down my back to cup my ass. He pulls me against him so his erection presses against the softest part of me. And then he does it again, grinding his hips and causing me to moan aloud.

"Oh." I gasp, tingles and butterflies running from the pads of my fingers to the tips of my toes.

Soren groans underneath me, pulling back to look at me. "Damn, girl."

"I want—" I pant.

"Yeah, me too." He smooths my hair back from my face. "But we don't have to rush into anything. We're not going anywhere. When you decide what you want, we'll be ready."

Just as quickly as he kisses me, he stops and rolls me off to his side, propping his head on his hand. Trailing his fingers down my arm and over my hip, his eyes don't exactly follow as his gaze traces over my breasts. "Anytime you want to kiss me, Leti, do it. I promise I'll want it."

Then he places a chaste kiss against my lips and stands, walking to the bedroom door. With his hand on the knob, he glances back at me with a smile. "I'm going to make a snack. We bought a couple of board games and a variety of paperbacks to entertain us. I can download any movie you want and play any song you can think of if you get the urge to dance for us. But whatever you do, don't hide away in here. Spend time with us and brighten our day, beautiful."

He closes the door behind him and I collapse on the bed, sliding my hands over my body, searching for the source of the itch I desperately need to scratch. I've been kissed senseless by two men in the span of an hour.

Should I be ashamed?

Should I go for three?

And if I do, can I bring myself to do more?

I hop off the bed and gather the bottles, taking them into the bathroom and placing them on the vanity. Then I sort through the t-shirts and shorts, amused that they are more Pip's style than my own. I would never wear shorts this tight or this short and yet, I'm excited about the attention these will bring me. I've shied away from the spotlight my entire life, but would it be so bad if I captured the notice of these three men?

Pulling off all the sales tags, I gather them and walk out of the bedroom in search of the washer and dryer. Caiden and Reese are standing in the kitchen and stop their conversation with their eyes fixed on me.

"I thought I would wash these." I hold up my bundle as evidence.

Caiden motions toward the garage. "The washer is this way."

I throw Reese a smile, hoping to convey my apologies without words—especially since I'm no longer allowed to say them. He visibly exhales and smiles back, tilting his head and telling me to follow Caiden into the washroom.

Caiden opens the washer lid and steps aside without saying a word. He doesn't have to—the look on his face says it all. He knows everything and is gauging my feelings, waiting patiently for me to do something. I throw my clothes in and then push him against the door, pressing my lips against his with a lot more confidence than I did last night. He doesn't hesitate, sliding his hands down my ass and lifting me into his arms. Turning us around, he presses my back against the door as I hook my ankles around his hips.

"That's my girl," Caiden growls, nibbling and then gently sucking my lower lip into his mouth before releasing it to trail kisses down my neck. I throw my head back, banging my skull against the door, but I don't care because he feels too good. "Fuck, the things I want to do to you."

My heart soars with his words. I've never been talked to this way, and I love it. I love being desired by them without reservation or fear of impropriety. These three men know exactly what they want—me—and they are not afraid to let me know it.

The door to the garage jerks behind us, bumping us forward. Caiden steps back with me wrapped around him and grins when Soren walks through the door. For a second, my heart stops and a wave of guilt washes over me. I kissed Soren five minutes ago. Reese, an hour ago. It's one thing if they say they're okay with me kissing all of them, but having one walk in while I'm with another feels like a betrayal.

Soren's eyes move from me to Caiden and back to me again. Then he leans forward and kisses my cheek before speaking to Caiden. "You could have helped me bring in the bags."

"But then I wouldn't be kissing Leti," Caiden replies with the biggest smile on his face.

Soren snorts and rolls his eyes before brushing past us. "Ass munch."

"He's not mad?" I whisper.

"Why would he be mad?" Caiden gives me a genuinely confused shake of his head and lowers me to the ground.

"I don't know—because I was kissing him five minutes ago."

Caiden leans forward and kisses my temple. "Don't think, beautiful. Do whatever feels good to you. I promise, none of us will be mad." He smacks my butt playfully. "I'll start washing your clothes. Why don't you go check out the games and books we bought?"

ENTES TUERE
PUNIRE IMPIOS

Chapter Twelve

LETI

I'VE SPENT many hours over the last four days kissing, touching, and cuddling Reese, Caiden, and Soren. I've initiated physical contact every time I've caught one of them alone, often hugging them when they least expect it, but also in front of each other while we play a game or watch a movie on the sofa.

Outside of a few minutes when I'm either using the bathroom or showering, I've had physical contact with someone. After days of hand holding, kissing, and fondling over my clothes, I'm now thoroughly frustrated and desperate for more.

Only, I don't know how to ask them for it.

The ache between my legs is excruciating, and my breasts are full and heavy after having my nipples teased through the thin cotton of my T-shirts. I've flounced around in the short shorts they bought me, trying my best imitation of Pip and her sassy swagger and inescapable sex appeal to no avail.

These men are rocks, sticking to their word to welcome anything I initiate, but not pressuring me for more.

I really wish they would pressure me for more.

I'm sitting in Reese's lap while we watch a movie. Caiden is in the kitchen, grabbing us a couple of drinks while Soren sits at a small desk in the corner with his computers.

I stare at Reese's hard jawline and sharp features, which are at complete odds with his gentle touch.

"What are you thinking, doll?" he says without taking his eyes off the TV.

Nuzzling his neck, I bring my mouth to his ear. "I want more."

He pulls back to look me in the eye, his voice dropping an octave. "What kind of more?"

"I ache."

A low growl comes from his chest. "Between your legs?"

I nod, a blush hitting my cheeks.

"You want me to take care of that for you?"

I nod again.

"Here on the couch, or do you want to go to the bedroom?"

At that moment, Caiden walks up and sets down two iced teas. My blush deepens, which is stupid. I could easily be asking Caiden or Soren for this, and although I've been making out with each of them in front of the others, I've yet to be with two of them at the same time.

Never mind three.

Honestly, I'm still unsure of how that would work.

"You don't have to stop talking because Caiden can hear you. Tell us what you want."

"I..." My gaze bounces between them and then I look over at the computer desk, realizing Soren's attention is off his screens and on me, too.

"She wants to come," Reese tells Caiden.

"Thank fucking Christ." Caiden blows out his breath, as if he's been holding it for days. "Is that what you want, baby? Do you want to come?"

I nod and say nothing.

"Clothes on or off?" Reese says.

"I..." Once again, I'm at a loss for words. I still haven't stripped in front of them, even though I'm wearing the least amount of clothing I've worn in my life.

"How about a compromise?" Caiden arches a brow. "We'll take off your shirt and shorts, but leave whatever you have underneath in place. We can work around them for the first time."

"Okay."

Caiden gathers the hem of my T-shirt, waiting patiently for me to lift my arms. Then he slides my shorts down my legs, laying them on my T-shirt over the sofa next to Reese's head. His eyes trail over my body, caressing me, making me feel worshiped. "Damn."

Reese runs his big hand up my side and cups my breast, pinching my lace-covered nipple between his thumb and forefinger, while Caiden slides his hands up the inside of my thighs, his touch gentle and loving. He rubs the crook of his finger over the lace covering my lower lips, where all the tingles accumulate every time one of them touches me.

Something about his gentle, unhurried touch has me spreading my legs, welcoming and inviting him in to play.

He chuckles. "That's our girl. Spread wide for me, and I'll make you feel good." His fingertips play along the edges of my panty line before pushing them inside, his skin making contact with my most sensitive spot, which he circles with the pad of his thumb.

"Ahhh," I croon before Reese seals my lips with his mouth, swallowing my cries of pleasure.

I'm arching into Reese's touch, kissing him with uncontrolled desire while Caiden kisses the insides of my thighs and uses his fingers to pleasure me. The pressure of my orgasm builds quickly as he circles my sensitive nub over and over and just when I think I'm about to come, he slides a long finger inside me, stroking me in rhythm with his thumb.

"Ahhh," I cry out, the sound muffled by Reese's tongue, my hips jerking against Caiden's hand.

I've never come with a man before.

I don't own any toys, and have only made myself come a handful of times over the years—usually when a steamy book makes the ache between my legs impossible to ignore—which is why I generally avoid reading them.

I'm not a prude—I swear, I'm not—but no one has ever inspired me to want more. I figured I'd meet the right man one day, and he'd turn on all the right faucets, stoke the fire that is supposed to burn deep inside me, but

I never expected to meet three men who stimulate my most basic needs.

I come back to myself when Reese lets go of my lips, and then glance down my body to find Caiden's face within inches of my most intimate of places. He pulls his finger out of me and brings it to his mouth, sucking my juices from his skin. "Mmmm. You taste good, baby. Have you ever tasted yourself?"

I can't believe he did that. It's carnal and intimate, and makes my belly clench with a desire for more. With wide eyes, I shake my head. "No."

"Has anyone?"

"No."

"Never?" Reese asks incredulously.

Again with the head shaking. Matt never did anything more than kiss me, lay me on my back, enter me, thrust a couple of times, and then tell me he loved me as he came. That was it. It was passionless, albeit gentle, and utterly devoid of emotion outside of his spoken words.

"Oh, baby. I know we said we wouldn't pressure you, but you have to let us go down on you." Caiden bites his finger, as if the idea of being denied physically hurts him.

Right now I'm feeling so good, I'd do anything they asked me. "What do I do?"

Caiden stands and offers me his hand. "Come sit on my lap and let Soren pleasure you."

I never heard Soren move, but he's sitting next to us on the coffee table, watching intently.

I turn my wide eyes to him. "Is that what you want?"

He nods and slides the back of his hand across his

mouth. "The idea of eating your pussy makes my mouth water."

Pussy. I haven't heard Soren use a crude word once and yet, right now, the word seems perfect, given the situation.

Giving Caiden my hand, I let him bring me to my feet and follow him to the armchair. He sits and pulls me to stand in front of him, hooking his fingers into the lacy legs of my panties. "I'm going to take these off now."

I nod, pushing them down my hips as he guides them past my knees before I step out of them. Then he pulls me onto his lap, my back pressed against his chest. "Relax, baby, and let us take care of you."

Soren stands between our knees and leans forward, kissing me on the mouth. His kiss is once again possessive, firm and dominant, and I'm melting into Caiden even though it's Soren turning me into a puddle of goo.

He pulls back slightly and whispers in my ear, "Thank you for this gift, beautiful."

Then he drops to his knees, peppering my thighs with kisses before putting his mouth between my legs. I'm instantly arching my back, my clit plump and sensitive from Caiden's touch minutes ago. The clasp on the front of my bra pops open with a flick of Reese's fingers, my breasts exposed as Soren's tongue plunges between my slick folds.

Caiden tilts my head back. "Kiss me, baby."

I do, overwhelmed with sensations as each man touches me, seeking my pleasure and taking nothing for himself. Caiden has one hand in my hair, pulling my head back, the other cupping my breast. Reese stands over us, his fingers dancing lightly over my skin, plucking and pulling at my nipple before letting go to once again caress my flesh. Soren is the most forceful of the three of them, pushing my thighs up to run his tongue over my... oh my god!

I yelp, and Caiden chuckles, pulling back to smile at me. "Did Soren tongue your asshole?"

"That was on purpose?"

"Yeah. You want him to do it again?"

Soren, whether he's listening or not, continues on, using his beard to scratch the itch building under his masterful touch. His fingers plunge in and out of me at an unhurried pace as he sucks my clit into his mouth. And then he changes it up, running his tongue from my asshole to my clit again.

My eyes must grow wide because Caiden chuckles again. "You want to know what being with the three of us would be like, baby? Sometimes it would be like this —your three men devouring you, pleasuring you, pampering you, tending to your every need. Sometimes it would be one-on-one, where we would make love until the early hours. But sometimes you'd have one of us in your mouth, one of us in your pussy, and one of us in your ass. If you were ours, there's nowhere we wouldn't touch you. No way we wouldn't claim you. We'd devote every second to your pleasure, making sure you came over and over again. You would be ours in every way."

Reese leans over me and claims my lips in a sweet

kiss. "We'll never force you, but know that we want you as ours and we're willing to wait for you."

Their words hit me deep and then are lost in a fog as Soren once again sucks my clit into his mouth and sends me rocketing over the edge. I whine and moan as I writhe against Caiden's body, riding Soren's skilled tongue, my orgasm causing my insides to spasm with my release.

ENTES TUERE
PUNIRE IMPIOS

FUCK, she tastes like heaven, and the way she comes satisfies all my fantasies.

I wipe my mouth and move up her body, sealing her mouth with my own. She moans, threading her fingers into my hair and pulling me closer. "Now you've tasted yourself, beautiful. Don't you taste good? Our sweet, beautiful girl."

I don't wait for her to answer me, reclaiming her lips in a possessive kiss, not giving one good fuck that Caiden is trapped underneath her. We've talked about this over and over again, promising we'd let her set the pace, even if we gently nudged her in our direction with every touch and caress. It's been the most frustrating and exciting four days of my life.

Will she pick us?

She's coming out of her shell quickly, given the circumstances that brought her to us. I think it's a combination of her need to be loved and showered with affection and our desire to do exactly that.

She's perfect for us.

Our sweet, beautiful girl, desperate to be adored and praised.

I pull back, smiling at her love-drunk expression. "Good girl."

She giggles. "Why do I like it so much when you say that?"

"Because, deep down, you hear all the subtext behind those words." I kiss her forehead and take a couple steps back, my thoughts diverted when my computer beeps with a pre-programmed alert designed to get my undivided attention.

Exchanging a glance with Caiden and Reese, I turn back to my monitors and the program I designed to back-trace the MAC address monitoring the tracker from the scrambler Claudine installed, which lets me know when it's online.

Her signal is broadcasting, pinging and searching in an area near Lee's team. I run a trace log and find she's been popping hot for thirty or so seconds every twenty minutes for the last three hours, inching closer to their location with every sweep.

I bring up my map, triangulating the signals and calculating them to be within a few miles of Alpha-3 team's secure location. Grabbing my phone, I turn to find Reese lifting Leti off Caiden's lap, sliding her shorts up her long legs.

"Something wrong?" Caiden raises his brow.

I wave our secure phone and tuck my tablet under my arm, but shake my head because I don't want to say anything that might upset Leti. "Nothing much. I need to make a quick call."

Walking out of the house, I go to the garage and dial the other team's secure line. The phone rings a couple times before Lee answers, slightly out of breath.

"Yeah?"

"You have visitors," I say, glancing at my tablet and shaking my head. I should have been paying attention. I wrote the program so it would send an audible alert when the trace broached a five-mile radius of either of our secure locations or the Krushner estate, but if I'd been watching, I would have seen her circling hours ago. "They're within five miles of your position."

"Five miles?" I hear the alert and annoyance in Lee's voice while Porter chatters behind him.

I rub my beard, Leti's scent fresh on my whiskers. "Yeah, I'm sorry I didn't catch it sooner. They started pinging something at your location about three hours ago, coming online for a few seconds before taking themselves back offline for another twenty minutes. From what I can tell, they've narrowed down your position from a fifty to a five-mile radius in seven pings. The only thing I can think of is you are broadcasting something now that you weren't over the last few days."

"Fuck," Lee growls. "Okay. Thanks for the heads up."

"I'll see what I can do about getting a visual of your location and will send you something as soon as I can."

"Thanks, Soren." Lee hangs up on me at the same time Reese walks into the garage.

"What's up?"

"Claudine popped hot after being dark for four days, and they are within five miles of Lee's team." I can barely make eye contact with Reese as my failure to be properly prepared weighs on me.

Reese exhales, leaning his ass against the tool bench and crossing his arms over his chest. "This is about to be over."

He doesn't berate me, and where his thought process goes surprises me. "You don't know that."

"I feel it in my bones. Lee, Case, and Porter will end it this evening, and we'll be sleeping in our own beds tonight." He glances at the house, but I know what he's really doing is looking at the walls surrounding Leti. "All of us."

"What are we going to do?" We can't let her go, not when we are this close to making her ours.

"We're going to finish the job and tell her exactly how we feel. Then we're going to let her go."

Closing my eyes, I lean against the hood of our Suburban. "Just like that?"

"We can't keep her caged forever," Reese says, and something about his tone makes me open my eyes. This hurts him as deeply as it cuts me. While not ideal, I've rather enjoyed playing house in the suburbs with our sweet girl as she blossoms into the confident, loving, unapologetic, self-assured woman she should have been all along.

"Now that we've awoken something in her, she knows what she's missing, but she has to be free to choose us." He nods, more to himself as if he's having an internal debate, than to me. "She'll choose us, but we have to give her time."

I sigh. "For obvious reasons, we've handled her with kid gloves since meeting her, but if we're going to let our little bird go, then she has to understand what she's coming back to if she does choose us. No more hour-long make out sessions where we pass her around like a baby doll. Yes, we want to spoil her, but after this is over, it has to be on our terms. No more coddling. No more manipulating her into taking and giving a little more each time. If she comes to us, she has to know who we really are—all the time."

"So, we invite her to the club and let her see what being with the three of us is all about." Reese brings his dark eyes up to meet mine, the set line of his jaw telling me he understands and agrees with my point.

Nodding, I rub my hand over my face, inhaling her scent. "The club. That's about as raw as we get."

"Exactly."

ONE HOUR LATER, I'm packing my computer equipment after we received a SITREP from Alpha-3's team about their takedown of a tan Chevy van and one Claudine Humphreys. Caiden is ecstatic because Case confirmed putting a bullet between Joe Dawson's eyes. The douchebag pulled a weapon on one of the top marksmen in the world, and that didn't work out too well for him.

"Why are you packing your computers?" Leti walks in fresh from her shower and wraps her arms around me from behind. I stand and slide my hands over hers, interlacing our fingers. Closing my eyes, I bask in this moment, knowing it's about to come to an end.

A temporary end, hopefully, but a break in the cycle of touching that I'm not going to enjoy.

Reese comes out of one of the bedrooms. "Hey, doll. Come sit with us."

I squeeze her hands and turn to face her, brushing my thumb over her cheekbone where the bruises have lightened considerably. They are still there, though, as is the small cut on her lip and the yellowing bruise on her leg. She's never complained once about any of it. Never once bemoaned her battered face or said kissing with a split lip hurt in any way.

And besides the very first night while napping on the couch, she's given us no indication of bad dreams.

As I told her before, she is the strongest woman I've ever met.

I tilt my head to the sofa and give her a flirty wink, encouraging her to do as she's told.

She smiles, raises up on her toes, and kisses me chastely before turning and skipping over to Reese, plopping down on his lap. Caiden sits on the other end of the couch, and I take residence between them on the coffee table.

"What's going on?" She glances between the three of us but settles her eyes on me.

"The other team has apprehended Claudine Humphreys and her accomplices."

Her eyes grow wide. "Is Pip okay?"

"She's fine. Everyone is fine." Caiden reaches out and rubs her calf. "They're dealing with the local law enforcement right now, and then they will pack and head home... which is what we need to do."

"Oh." Leti lowers her head, as if she finally understands the somber mood surrounding her. "What about her accomplices?"

What about Dawson? That is what she really means.

"They dealt with them. You won't have to worry about them anymore," Reese says as he slides his hand up and down her arm.

She smiles, but it's not a friendly one. It's one born of waning patience. "What does that mean?"

I shake my head at Caiden, knowing his delivery will be too upbeat for the story. Even though Joe brutalized her, nothing about what she's said to date says she has bloodlust. Will hearing about his death upset her? Maybe. There are people in the world that don't believe in capital punishment, exacted vengeance, or eye-for-an-eye vigilante justice regardless of being victimized.

Obviously, she's surrounded by three men who not only believe in it, but profit from it.

"I assume you're asking about the man who assaulted

you? They killed him when he pulled a gun on Alpha-3 team. You will never see him again."

She visibly sags against Reese—and damn, I wish I was the one holding her right now. "Good."

Caiden grins like a loon. "That's what I said."

Actually, he pumped his fists in the air and danced around the garage chanting, *fuck that motherfucker, I hope he burns in hell.*

"And the others?" she prods.

"The frat boy, as you called him, is Brad Mathews, and they shot him while approaching the property. He's critically injured and on his way to the ER. Claudine was arrested without issue. You'll have to deal with her if this case goes to trial, but if we can help you avoid being face to face with her, we will."

"I don't have a problem testifying against her." She shrugs. "Actually, I think I'd like to make eye contact with her again."

I reach out and squeeze her knee. "That's our strong girl."

"So, we're going home?" she asks.

"Your father wants to see you, and I'm sure your sister is ready to give you that hug she promised."

That makes her smile, but she ducks her chin and casts her eyes to her lap. "What does it mean for us?"

Reese cups her face, bringing her eyes to his. He kisses her gently before turning her head toward me. I lean forward and also kiss her softly, begrudgingly pulling back for Caiden to do the same.

"This has been an emotional week for you, Leti,"

Reese starts. "And while we want you, we aren't sure you are in the right mental state to make a decision about how you feel about us."

"So," Caiden sighs, "we think it would be best to go home for a couple of days, settle back into your life, and think about what you want when it comes to us."

I rub her thigh. "Like I told you a couple of days ago... we're not going anywhere. Go home and reconnect with your sister. Think about us and what you want. We'll be waiting."

"I'm sad." She tries to smile with tears in her eyes and I swear my heart is shredding itself right now.

I sink to my knees in front of her and put my head in her lap. "Me too, beautiful. But if we kept you, we'd be no better than the people who kidnapped you."

"Do you understand?" Reese asks.

Leti runs her fingers through my hair, petting me gently. "I understand."

ENTES TUERE
PUNIRE IMPIOS

Chapter Fourteen

LETI

I'VE BEEN HOME for nine days, and in some ways it's been wonderful. Pip was true to her word, and we've spent a lot of time getting to know each other again. We shop, we have lunch, and almost every other night, we have dinner with our father, who is trying to make up for lost time. Some of our conversations have been hard, and there have been a lot of tears shed, but I feel closer to them than ever.

And yet, with all the love floating around our home, I feel hollow and more alone than ever. I miss Caiden, Soren, and Reese. I miss touching and being touched by them. My mind swims with thoughts of them and the gentle way they cared for me.

But it's more than that. They woke something dormant in me—something I was afraid I would never feel. There was a time I thought I was defective, not wanting the things girls my age should want. Sex, intimacy, filthy carnal pleasures—I dream of it now, fantasies so vivid, I wake up soaking wet and pulsating with an unfettered desire coursing through my veins.

Dare I say? I'm horny.

I want to be claimed by my men.

I want to be thoroughly fucked and pleasured.

I want this need banging around inside of me satiated.

I've only heard from Caiden, and that was via an old-fashioned notecard sent through USPS. Pen to paper, his penmanship was beautiful, his words precise and elegant.

WE MISS YOU.
WE WANT YOU.
WE LOVE YOU.

I didn't know how to respond, not that there was a physical address for me to mail a letter to. There was a business card with a phone number and nothing more. I thought about calling it, but what would I say?

Come get me.

That's what I want to say, but I'm scared. What would my father think? What would Pip say? How does a relationship like this work in society? Do I really care?

"You've got mail." Pip comes into the kitchen where I'm nursing a cup of coffee and hands me a sleek black envelope.

I frown and open it, my cheeks turning rosy as my eyes skim the card stock.

Our lifestyle is not traditional,
and it's not for the faint of heart.
One thing we didn't talk with you about
was our membership at The Access Club.
If you are unaware, The Access Club is a sex club
where people with untraditional appetites
can relax with like-minded individuals.
We've been members for years,
but we've never had a pet of our own to share it with us.

Nothing would make us happier to share it with you.

Trust us to protect you.
Trust us to take care of you.
Trust us to love you.
Choose us.

Come to The Access Club Saturday night, nine p.m.
We'll be waiting for you—always.

All our love, Caiden, Reese, and Soren

INSIDE IS a business card with an address, but no name.

"Is it a party invite?" Pip sits across from me with her own cup of coffee.

Folding the card and sliding it back into the envelope, I bite my lip and make eye contact with my sister. I can't believe I'm about to have this conversation with her, but if not her, who? "You've been all around the world. Can I ask you a crazy question?"

"Of course." She reaches across the table and rubs my hand. "You can ask me anything."

"No judgment?"

She laughs. "Absolutely."

I chew on my cheek, my eyes bouncing around the room as I put my thoughts into words. "Have you ever heard of a woman dating more than one man?"

"Sure."

"No, I mean, dating them at the same time." I twist my fingers around each other to emphasize my point. "Like together."

"How many men?"

I blush. "Let's say three."

Pip giggles. "It's not common, but not unheard of either. Some people call it a reverse harem, some people call it polyamory. What they call it really depends on the group's dynamics in and out of the bedroom. Why?"

My eyes go to the sleek black invitation. "Promise you won't tell anyone?"

"You're my sister. Your confidence is mine to keep, and vice versa."

I take a deep breath, exhaling it slowly, my cheeks turning a fire engine red. "Something happened with Reese, Caiden, and Soren."

"What?" Pip's tone is sharp and judgmental.

I shake my head and drop my eyes to my lap. "Nevermind."

Pip pulls my hand across the table, forcing me to look at her. "Did you want something to happen with them?"

"Yes." A stray tear falls from my eye. "I know it's wrong, and I know I'm weird, but I think I love them."

She shakes her head. "It's not wrong, and you're not weird, and I completely understand because something happened between me, Lee, Case, and Porter."

My eyes grow as wide as dinner plates. "Really?"

She motions to the black envelope. "Is that a note from them?"

"They want me to meet them Saturday night."

"Go." Pip nods enthusiastically.

"How can I?"

"Oh, Leti. I've been all around the world and introduced to all kinds of people, and the one thing I can tell you is happiness is fleeting, but finding someone to love you the way you want to be loved is special—a once-in-a-lifetime style special. If you found three men who want to love you, whom you also love—well, you've hit the jackpot, and you can't turn your back on it, regardless of what is considered a societal norm."

"What about your men? Have you heard from them?"

She glances down and shakes her head. "No, not yet."

"Do you want to, Pip?"

"Yes, but I'm afraid. What if they don't want me?"

I roll my eyes. "Of course they want you. You're amazing and vivacious and maybe a bit of a handful."

She chuckles. "I think they like that last part the most."

I hold up my hand, showing Pip how it shakes. "Look at me, I'm so nervous. I don't think I can do this."

She grabs my hand and squeezes it. "I tell you what. If you go on this date with them, I'll track down my men and let them know how I feel. We'll both be putting ourselves out there, supporting each other while we do one of the scariest things in our lives."

"Yeah?" My eyes fill with tears. Happy tears, but tears nonetheless.

"Yeah." Pip spreads her arms wide, offering me a hug. "Now, let's go shopping and buy you an amazing dress for your date."

IT'S Saturday night and I'm wearing the sexiest, slinkiest, most revealing full-length gown I've ever seen off the red carpet. This is so Pip, and yet, I feel glamorous wearing it.

Pip walks me out of the house and nods, sliding her hands up my bare arms. "You look amazing. They are going to eat their tongues when they see you."

"I wish it was cold enough to wear a cape or something. I feel so exposed." I fidget, even though there isn't nearly enough fabric to adjust.

"Stop." She giggles. "You look amazing. Have fun. Be honest with yourself and let them love you."

I pull her into my arms. "I couldn't do this without your support. Thank you."

"Hey, what's a sister for?"

Giggling, I ignore the way the town car driver's eyes bug out of his head when he looks at us. "I love you, Pip."

"I love you, too." She squeezes me and then pushes me toward the open door. "Now go get your men."

ENTES TUERE
PUNIRE IMPIOS

Chapter Fifteen

I NEVER CLAIMED to be a poet, but I hope my invitation sparks a sense of adventure in Leti and gives her the strength to come to us tonight.

We're sitting in a booth, nursing a couple of whiskeys, and watching the small crowd grow. It's early for The Access Club, but I felt the smaller crowd would make her more comfortable, even though we have no intention of hanging out with the masses any longer than necessary.

We have a room reserved, but we'll only go inside if she comes.

We have no indication if she'll make it or not.

No word from her.

No phone calls.

It would have been easy enough for Soren to do some of snooping. He could have easily hacked her phone and turned it into a listening device, but that wouldn't have made all of this waiting any easier.

Instead, the three of us are suited up with silk ties—

which makes my cock hard as a rock—and doing our best to not appear antsy.

I glance at my watch to find it's ten after nine. "She's not going to show."

"She is," Reese says.

"She's late," I grumble.

"We'll forgive her." Reese slides his eyes my way and then diverts his gaze over my shoulder, hissing under his breath. "Fuck me."

I turn to look over my shoulder at the hostess as she escorts Leti to our table in a painted-on dress with sheer panels, leaving very little to the imagination. "Oh, fuck."

Scrambling to my feet, I suck in my breath as Soren steps forward and offers her his hand.

Smiling, Leti keeps her head down, but looks up at us through her lashes.

Shyness warring with excitement—I hope.

"You look beautiful." He pulls her close and kisses her cheek.

Reese walks around me and takes her other hand, lifting it to his mouth. "Hey, doll. I knew you'd come."

She brings her eyes to me and squeaks, "Hi."

I push Reese out of the way and pull her into my arms. Bracing her lower back with my forearm, I bend her backward and claim her lips like I want to claim every other part of her. She melts in my arms, moaning when I slide my tongue into her mouth. Massaging her tongue with mine, I tell her everything I have to say with this one kiss.

I missed you.

I love you.

Don't ever leave me again.

Reese smacks my shoulder and speaks directly into my ear. "You're making a spectacle of yourself."

I pull back and smile. "Let people look. They're jealous I'm kissing the most beautiful woman here."

She smiles. "I missed you."

Growling, I stand with her in my arms and pull her tight against my body. "I missed you more."

I can't take my hands off of her. It's like if I do, she'll disappear. I guide her to the empty chair between Soren and me and sit beside her.

Reese shakes his head, a sly grin on his face. "Ass munch."

"Yeah, I know." My gaze roams over her body, drinking in every inch of her.

"This isn't exactly like watching movies and playing board games." Leti motions to the room with a wave of her hand. "What do you do here?"

I lift my drink. "Normally we sit back, watch, and have a couple of drinks."

"Sometimes we do more." Soren says softly.

"You have sex with women here?" she murmurs.

Reese takes a deep breath. "We have."

"Really?" Her voice cracks and I know this upsets her.

Dammit. The last thing I want to do is upset her. But Reese and Soren are right. We have to present her with exactly who we were and who we are, so when she enters a relationship with us, she's fully informed.

Yes, we've had sex with women here.

No, none of them meant anything more than a good time. Everyone enjoyed themselves, but there was no lasting connection. Nothing like the feelings we have for her.

"I told you, doll, we don't lie. Ever." Reese takes a deep drink out of his glass.

"In a relationship like ours, it's important to be honest with each other." Soren holds her hand on his thigh.

She nods, her eyes bouncing around the room. "Are any of the women you've had sex with here now?"

Fuck me. She would ask us that.

"The hostess," I sigh. "A couple of months ago."

"The one who escorted me to the table?" Her eyes grow wide.

"Yeah. We don't normally engage with the staff, but we've known her for a long time."

"Do you—" she bites her lip "—care for her?"

"No more than we care for a friend. She had an itch, and that night she asked us to scratch it. It meant nothing more than four consenting adults having a good time," Reese says.

"Baby," I stroke her cheek with my thumb. "We've never felt about anyone the way we feel about you. I've never told a woman I love her outside of my mother and my sister, and maybe an aunt. But I love you. I knew the moment I held you in my arms that you were going to be mine. Ours. Not just for tonight, or for a month, but forever."

She leans into my hand. "I want to be yours—all of yours."

"Forever?"

Soren leans in and kisses her neck. "Hmmm, forever sounds good to me."

"Okay, this is bullshit," Reese grumbles. He stands and grabs her hand, hauling her out of her chair, sitting down, and pulling her back into his lap—so she's sandwiched between the three of us, like she should be.

She giggles, snuggling into his chest. "Were you lonely over there?"

"Yes." He kisses her cheek.

Leti's gaze bounces between the three of us. "So... people have sex here at the club?"

"Yes," Reese says again.

"Where?"

"Mostly in the rooms upstairs," Soren answers her.

"Do we have a room?"

I blow out the breath I've been holding and ask my question again. "Will you be ours forever?"

She nods. "I will."

I smile. "Then we have a room upstairs."

"Maybe we should go check it—"

I'm on my feet and pulling her to hers before she can finish her thought, my arm wrapped around her waist. I don't give Reese or Soren a second glance, expecting them to catch up as I move her across the room and through the crowd to the stairs. Every man in this place gawks at our queen, but I don't care.

She's mine.

She's ours.

And tonight, we'll claim her forever.

Reese and Soren catch up as we ascend the stairs and walk as a precise military unit to our room. I pull the key from my pocket and disengage the lock, pushing the door open. Leti steps through the threshold, and I'm sure she's nervous, but our strong girl tamps down any embarrassment she feels and holds her head high.

Our room is a comfortable suite with a living area and a wet bar, a few toys and other tame accessories. The bedroom is off to the left. It has an oversized king bed with an ensuite to include a massive shower and a jacuzzi tub. Many people come with their own bag of tricks, but one can also order a la carte. We went for comfort and privacy tonight, and ordered a pamper kit to include robes, extra towels, bath salts, bubbles, and strawberry-scented lube.

I know, I know... I'm a sap. But I know this will be her first time doing anything remotely non-vanilla. I mean, Soren is the one and only man to go down on her and eat her pretty pussy, something I plan to do tonight. Even though some jackass took her virginity, he never really claimed her, giving her exactly zero orgasms for her troubles.

Tonight will be special. I already know it will be for us, and I'm willing to go full sap and write her name in rose petals if it touches her heart and makes her melt.

She glances around, taking in the luxurious furniture. "Wow. This is a lot nicer than I imagined."

I slide behind her and run my hands up her arms. "We wouldn't take you to some place unfit for a queen."

"Have you been in this room before?" She glances over her shoulder at me.

"No." Reese steps beside her and takes her hand, leading her to the wet bar and away from my arms. "We wouldn't share you in a room with memories of anyone else."

"We'll be wiping and replacing everything before you with new memories, anyway," Soren says, shutting and locking the door behind him.

She flashes a demure smile, her eyes bouncing from Reese to me, and then to Soren. "How do we begin?"

ENTES TUERE
PUNIRE IMPIOS

Chapter Sixteen

I'M NERVOUS, but I also want this more than air.

Their truthfulness is awe-inspiring. Most men would have lied when asked if they'd had sex with anyone at the club—but not my men, and I wouldn't have it any other way.

"We start with a kiss." Caiden puts his finger under my chin and lifts my face, kissing me much more gently than he did at the table ten minutes ago. But it doesn't matter if it's gentle, because I melt into him just the same.

"While this dress is beautiful, it is too delicate for what we want to do." Soren comes up from behind me, sliding the straps off my shoulders.

This dress fits like a glove, and that's because it's mostly spandex. It hugs and highlights every little curve I have, but it's not nearly as delicate as it looks, which he finds out as he pushes it down past my breasts to my waist. Soren spins me around to face him, one hand in my hair to cradle the back of my head, his other sliding down my bare back. He kisses me with the same level of possessive-ness that Caiden kissed me with on the club room floor.

Reese moves to the other side of me, his hand sliding up my belly to cup my breast. "I'm going to assume that since Soren was the first man to taste your pussy, you've also never held a man's cock in your mouth?"

Soren releases my lips, his eyes sliding to the left to draw my attention to Reese and his question. "No, I've never done that."

I glance at each of them, making sure to convey my absolute dedication to this and us with a look. "But I want to. I want to do everything with you."

"And you will, my love." Reese smiles. "You will."

He offers me his hand, pulling me out of Soren's arms and walking me to the arm of the couch. At the same time, he loosens his tie and pulls it free from his collar. "Put your hands right here and grip the arm of the couch."

When I throw him a questioning raise of my eyebrow, he shakes his head and smiles. "You have to trust us to take care of you and only do things you absolutely love. So, doll, do you trust us?"

I nod and place my hands where he tells me.

He kisses my temple and whispers in my ear. "Good girl."

From behind me, Soren pulls my dress and panties down until they pool at my feet. I'm completely naked, slightly bent over, and shivering with anticipation of what is coming.

I do trust these men.

I trust them with everything I have, including my heart.

But I have to admit, this is the first time I've ever been naked in front of a man. Fully naked. Where I'm not already underneath them, like I was at the safe house in Peoria. I would feel uncomfortable standing here in nothing, but the heat in Reese's eyes makes me believe I'm the most beautiful woman he's ever seen.

Someone places a kiss on my ass, and I turn around to see Caiden staring up at me, his tie also off and his shirt buttons undone. "Fuck, you are the tastiest morsel I've ever had my hands on."

He taps me lightly on the calf. "Step out of your dress and spread your legs for me."

I do as I'm told, widening my stance to be shoulder-width apart. I'm so exposed this way, but then Caiden drags his eyes from mine to my pussy, and purses his lips to blow air gently across my damp heat.

I let out a low moan.

"I'm going to taste you now, Leti. I'm going to fuck you with my tongue until you come into my mouth, and then I'm going to fuck you with my dick. That's what you want. That's why you're here with us. You need my tongue and cock deep inside of you, don't you, baby?"

I nod, my insides quivering with need. I've never wanted anything more in my life. This is what I thought it would be like. My sexual awakening is something I can't deny or ignore.

I prayed the man I loved would be the man to bring this need out of me.

I never expected it to be three men.

Soren comes up beside me, his chest and feet bare, his slacks unbuttoned and hanging low on his hips. He kneels on the cushion in front of me and leans forward to place a gentle kiss on my lips. "You are going to take my cock between your pretty lips first."

"I've never done this before," I whisper. "What if I do it wrong?"

"It's not possible to do this wrong." He grins and shakes his head, at the same time reaching into his slacks and pulling out his cock. With his hand flat between my shoulder blades, he pushes me down to where I am eye level with his erection. "Lean on your elbows and give me your hand."

Folding one arm underneath me, I hoist my breasts while reaching forward with my other hand, letting Soren wrap my fingers around his thick member. I'm instantly fascinated. It's both hard and soft at the same time.

He's so hard, I have to wonder how it's not painful?

Caiden takes this moment to grip and push my ass cheeks apart, sliding his tongue over my pussy and causing me to forget my question.

"Fuck me, you have a pretty pussy," Caiden says, at the same time as Soren chuckles and guides my hand up and down his length. "All you have to do is keep moving like this with your hand and your mouth. Keep your tongue as wet as possible and let nature take over."

He nods, encouraging me. "Go ahead."

Tentatively, I open my mouth and stick my tongue out, guiding him past my lips. A sharp intake of breath brings my eyes up, but the look of pure pleasure on his face encourages me to keep going. I slide him in and out of my mouth a couple of times, flexing my hand and trying to match my suction to the strength with which I grip him.

He wraps his fingers around mine again, squeezing them down. "You can't hurt me unless you decide to crunch down with your back molars. Keep going."

Then he releases my hand and slides his fingers into my hair, cupping the back of my head, encouraging me to go faster and harder.

"How's our girl?" Reese says from beside me.

Soren grunts, his hand fisting a handful of my hair. "She's a fucking natural."

"Good girl." Reese kisses my neck and trails his lips over my shoulder, making me tingle all over.

At the same time, Caiden plunges his tongue deep inside of my pussy, as if he was waiting for me to catch a rhythm with Soren, which I've now lost as I moan out loud, pleasure rippling up my spine.

The hotter Caiden gets me by lavishing my pussy, the harder I suck and pull on Soren's cock. It's like one man feeds my passion for the other, and I want to make Soren feel as good as Caiden makes me.

"Oh, sweet girl," Soren groans. "Your mouth is pure heaven."

"She tastes like heaven, too," Caiden growls, sucking

my clit into his mouth at the same time as he pumps two fingers in and out of me.

Reese nibbles on my shoulder, sliding his hand down my spine and using his middle fingertip to rub a cool, slippery liquid over my asshole. I know this will happen. Caiden told me it was part of claiming me and making me theirs, but I can't help but tense, despite finding it oddly pleasurable.

Caiden strokes my inner wall, and my insides quiver. "That's my girl. Come for me, baby."

I come apart at his command, panting as I hold Soren in my mouth, crying out my release.

He pulls his fingers out of me, and the pressure at my back entrance stops as well. Then Caiden is pressing the head of his cock against my pussy, pushing in slowly, stretching and filling me in the most delicious way. It feels so good. I arch my back, wordlessly asking him for more.

Then Soren flexes his hand in my hair, thrusting his hips forward and hitting the back of my throat, triggering my gag reflex.

"Sorry, beautiful, but you feel so good and I really want to fuck your pretty mouth."

Hearing Soren curse so freely lets me know how carnal kand intimate this moment is between us. I'm seeing a new side of him, and I guess he's seeing a new side of me. There is no room for shy or awkward behavior here. We are as raw as we can be right now.

I tighten my fist and pump him harder, faster, until

the tendons in his neck pop and he groans, "Oh, fuck. Yes. That's my beautiful baby girl."

The first shot of cum hits the back of my throat, and I will myself to relax, swallowing every drop he has for me without thought. He cups my cheeks and tilts my face up, leaning down to kiss my lips. "Damn, beautiful. You are amazing. That mouth of yours... you did such a good job. I'm so proud of you."

My entire body lights up under his praise, which only makes me want more.

Caiden shoves his hips forward, causing me to throw my head back and cry out. He grabs hold of my hair and pulls me off of my elbows, my head tilted back to rest upon his shoulder. Even with this new position, he doesn't stop the onslaught of his hips as they slam against my ass, pistoning his thick cock in and out of my pussy until he's grunting and hissing in my ear. "You're about to make me come, baby."

"Okay," I moan.

He crosses his forearm over my chest and covers my breast with his hand, his warm breath on my ear. "I'm going to shoot my cum deep inside you, baby, and mark you as mine."

Reese walks up to us and runs his finger from my belly button to my clit, rubbing it with a tender touch. "Are you protected, Leti?"

Are they asking about birth control? "I've been on the pill since I was seventeen to regulate my periods."

"Good. While the idea of you carrying our baby is

fucking hot, we want nothing stopping us from filling you with our cum tonight."

"Oh," I gasp as Caiden sucks my earlobe in between his teeth, his arm tightening as he grunts through his release.

Reese continues to rub my clit, bringing me to and keeping me on the edge until Caiden loosens his hold on me.

I whimper when he pulls his hand away. "More."

He grins and kisses me, pulling me away from Caiden and swinging me into his arms, carrying me like his bride into the bedroom. "We're going to give you more, baby."

I swoon and press my face into his neck.

I had no idea sex could feel like this.

I had no idea my entire body would vibrate with every touch.

I had no idea such loving words would fill my heart to the point it wants to burst.

I had no idea what I was missing.

ENTES TUERE
PUNIRE IMPIOS

I CARRY her into the bedroom. Soren is already there and in the process of removing his slacks. Caiden is stumbling in behind us, disorientated and high from coming. I'm the only one dressed, but it won't take me but five seconds to shed what's left of my damn suit.

And now you know why putting on a tie gets me hard.

Soren sits on the edge of the bed and puts his arms out, his cock hard again and ready to go. That's the thing about Soren... he might have been a late bloomer, but the man can go, and go, and go some more. I thought my stamina was impressive, but he's the fucking Energizer Bunny.

Literally—the Energizer fucking Bunny.

I put Leti down so her feet are on the floor, and then kiss her neck before turning her to face Soren, letting him guide her to where we all want her. Removing my cufflinks, I put them on top of the dresser with the small bottle of lube I pull out of my pocket. Within seconds, my shirt is off and thrown to the nearby chair.

Soren has Leti straddling him, and he's kissing her senseless, his fingertips digging into her ass. "You did so good. You're perfect for us. Our flawless, beautiful girl," he coos over and over again, keeping her love drunk.

Our girl loves to have affirming words and affection thrown at her, and unlike most men, the three of us happen to love to do it.

I shuck off my pants and fist my aching cock. I've jerked off dozens of times since meeting Leti and encouraging her to find comfort in us almost two weeks ago, but not one orgasm has brought me the release I was after. I want her like I've never wanted another. My brothers feel the same way, only solidifying she is the one for us.

Soren turns her head, so she's looking at me, her eyes locked onto my fist wrapped around my cock. He's whispering something in her ear, which causes her eyes to flare with heat, and her lips to spread in a smile.

I return her smile. "Do you want to suck my cock, baby?"

She licks her lips and nods. I take the two steps forward and line up the tip wet with pre-cum to her plump lips. She opens her mouth wide and sticks out her tongue flat, her eyes locked on mine.

Growling, I slide my cock over her tongue and cup her cheek. "What a doll. Perfect in every way."

Her mouth is heaven—my brother was not lying.

I close my eyes and tilt my head back, willing myself to hold back the orgasm begging to be set free. I feel like

I've gone a lifetime without being touched by anything other than my own hand. Not wanting to make a fool out of myself and come here and now, I pull free from her pouty lips and lean down to kiss her forehead. "How do you feel, doll?"

"Out of my head." She smiles.

"And?"

"I want more."

"Good girl. Lay down with Soren."

Soren swings her face back to him and lies back, pulling her down with him. "Lift up, beautiful." He says, lining up his cock with her opening and sliding in slowly.

She moans, arching her back. I slide my hand up her spine and push her shoulders down, while I pop open the bottle of lube and squeeze a couple of cool drops into the top of her ass crack. "Keep that ass up in the air, doll."

Starting with my thumb, I slide the lube all over her puckered rosette, applying pressure until she pushes back on me, my digit breaching the tight ring of muscle.

Some women hate this.

Some women tolerate it.

But some women, and I'm guessing Leti is one of them, absolutely love anal sex.

She gasps, holds still for a moment, and then pushes back for more.

"Good girl." I squirt a couple more drops of lube and work it in and out of her, swapping out my thumb for a finger, and then two, pushing a little deeper each time. She rolls her hips, riding my fingers while riding Soren's cock, and panting as Caiden comes in from the bathroom and kneels on the mattress, taking residence above their heads.

He runs his fingers through her hair and kisses the top of her head. "Look at you taking it so well from my brothers. Does it feel good, baby?"

"Mmhmmm." She nods and cries out as I pump faster and harder, prepping her for me.

"Are you ready for Reese to slide his cock inside of you?"

"Yes." She sounds desperate, and I couldn't be more pleased. It's always the quiet and shy ones that become the most uninhibited once they feel safe.

Pressing the head of my cock slick with lube against her tight hole, I lay my hand flat against the dip in her ass and push gently. At the same time, Soren pulls out. "Relax, doll."

She gasps, her muscles bunching for only a second before Soren slides his fingers over her clit, effectively dividing her attention. Caiden kisses her, cupping her cheeks in his big hands. "You're doing so good."

"Fuck," I hiss as I push past the tight ring of muscle, a sweat breaking out across my brow. "She's so tight."

"She's tight everywhere." Soren slips back inside her once I'm fully seated deep within her ass.

"Perfect in every way," Caiden says before swallowing her cries of pleasure with a kiss.

ENTES TUERE
PUNIRE IMPIOS

Chapter Eighteen

LETI

"DIDN'T I TELL YOU, BABY?" Caiden holds my head and looks at me with a possession and desire I've never known. Well, at least not before I met them. "When we claim you, we'll take you together, filling every hole you have. The four of us are going to become one. You belong to us, and we belong to you."

"Forever," I grunt as Soren and Reese coordinate their thrusts, one pulling out as the other pushes in and vice versa. They keep me deliciously full, on the verge of being overstuffed, pushing me toward and then backing me off the edge of crying no more with each slow slide of their cock.

"That's right," Caiden lines his cock up with my mouth and I open wide for him, offering him my tongue. "Forever."

I'm stuffed full, exactly like he said I would be two weeks ago. I wonder what we look like when coupled like this?

I feel loved and cherished, but do I look it?

Do I care?

Caiden smoothes my hair back from my lips, gathering it into a loose ponytail as he picks up rhythm and fucks my mouth. Soren digs his fingers into my hips, pressing his thumbs near my pubic bone, lifting his hips as he fucks me from underneath while Reese grips my waist, continuing his slow and steady assault on my ass.

They move in and out of me like a finely tuned unit, a push and pull symphony that has a different kind of orgasm building within me. No one is touching my clit, and yet I feel like I'm gushing wet, a pressure building low in my belly that makes me want to scream.

"That's our girl. Your pussy is clamping down on me, ready to milk me clean of my cum." Soren ducks his head and presses kisses on my collarbone before sucking my nipple into his mouth. My neck is stretched and exposed for him as Caiden keeps my head pulled back, my body contorted with my back arched, while all three of my men fill me.

"I'm going to come," Reese grunts, a light smack landing on my ass before he starts thrusting in and out of me harder and faster. Soren also speeds up, both men chasing their release, which only spurs on the pressure building low in my belly, making me insane with need.

Soren swipes his thumb over my clit once and it's like flicking a switch, the dam breaking and my body vibrating with my climax.

Something akin to "Oh my god, oh my god, oh my god" comes out as a garbled mess as Caiden also takes complete control, fucking my mouth and shooting his cum down my throat. He's the first to pull out, yanking my hair hard and kissing me with a possessiveness I feel in my toes. "Fucking love you, baby."

He releases my hair, letting me collapse on Soren as both he and Reese slow down, returning to slow, languid, alternating strokes. Soren slides his hands up my back and kisses me gently. "Good girl, filling yourself with our cum."

"I love you," I whisper, completely overwhelmed by the emotions rushing to the surface.

He smiles. "I love you, too."

Caiden climbs off the bed at the same time as Reese pulls out of my ass, the sudden loss of both of them causing my insides to clench around Soren—as if I'm desperate not to be abandoned.

Soren groans and then chuckles. "I'm not going anywhere, beautiful."

A warm, damp cloth caresses my ass, and I whip my head around to find Reese cleaning me before using the cloth on himself. He smiles and winks at me before tossing the washcloth into the corner. Then he lifts my boneless body off Soren and cradles me in his arms as he sits on the edge of the bed with me in his lap. He might have wiped me clean, but his and Soren's cum leaks out of my body onto his thigh in this seated position.

If he minds, he doesn't show it.

"How are you feeling, doll?"

I sigh and lean my head against his shoulder. "Full and complete."

"Mmmm." He nuzzles his face into my neck. "You take our cocks so good, it's like you were made for us."

"Maybe I was?"

Caiden kisses the other side of my neck and then sits next to us. "We've got some stuff to figure out, baby. Not tonight, but in general."

"What's that?"

"We want you with us. We want to wake up with you every morning—"

"And sink deep into your cunt every night," Reese growls in my ear.

Caiden reaches behind us and smacks the back of Reese's head, which knocks his forehead into my temple.

"Owww," I giggle.

"Sorry, baby." Caiden frowns at Reese. "Sooner rather than later, we need to figure out the logistics of our relationship, because I don't want to go another night without sleeping with you in my arms."

My mind goes to my father, which feels all kinds of wrong, given I'm naked with three men. I've remained close due to some unrequited obligation to take care of him after my mother died. He never asked me to shackle my life to him. If anything, he's pushed me to have my own life, like Pip. But things have been different over the last two weeks. He's tried to reconnect with us—tried to make up for lost time.

Pip. She might be having a night with her own three men right now. Are they asking her the same question? If so, how will she answer them?

Oh, my god—what will our father say?

As soon as the question comes to mind, I realize I don't care. It's time for me to focus on my happiness, my fulfillment, my pleasure. And to be honest, I don't think after tonight I could take a night away from their arms. The last week and a half without them has been torture. How did I become addicted to them so quickly?

"Baby?" Caiden claims my lips, plunging his tongue into my mouth. He kisses me senseless until I forget what I'm thinking about. "What's on your mind?"

"I can't remember."

He chuckles. "Good to know my kisses are effective."

Soren comes out of the bathroom with a fluffy robe over his forearm, the sound of water running behind him. "We don't have to sort this out now. Let's take a bath."

"I want to live with you," I blurt out, my eyes bouncing from Caiden to Reese to Soren and back to Caiden. "I really do."

"Oh, baby." Caiden cradles my face and kisses me. "You've made us so happy."

"Thrilled." Soren turns my head and also kisses me.

"You've given us an amazing gift." Reese kisses my shoulder, love infusing me from all sides.

"What gift is that?" Sitting on Reese's lap, I squeeze Caiden's hand and smile at Soren.

"Family."

ENTES TUERE
PUNIRE IMPIOS

LETI

"Where are you?" My father has called multiple times tonight, and I finally had to leave my men to answer my phone.

"Hi?" my voice squeaks as I prepare yet another lie. I suck at lying, something that Pip likes to tease me about regularly. We've become close while perusing our own lives at the same time. I think if only one of us had found love with three men, we wouldn't have the relationship we have now. I mean, I know I wouldn't have had the nerve to pursue my relationship without Pip's support. And I'm betting she wouldn't have told me about her relationship if I wasn't going through the same thing. She would have thought it was too out-of-the-norm for someone like me, and would have avoided telling me things that she thought would upset me.

Considering I'd never heard of such an arrangement

prior to meeting my men, I guess she would have been somewhat right.

"I haven't seen you in a few days," my father says. "I was hoping me and my girls could have dinner, but Pip's not answering my calls either."

"Oh, Dad," I sigh. "I'll call her. When would you like to have dinner?"

"I wanted to have it last night, and then tonight, but I guess I will settle for tomorrow. Where are you?"

"Uh…" I shake my head at Caiden, who stalks toward me with a predatory gleam in his eye. He just got out of the shower, his hair wet and dripping onto his shoulders. "I'm not coming home tonight."

"Yes, my daughter, I noticed that. You haven't slept in your bed all week." My father sighs. We are at this weird place in our relationship. After ten years of him having no idea where I am from one week to the next, he's now acutely aware of where I am—or in this case—where I am not at nighttime. "I wish you'd tell me what's going on. I know it's none of my business. You are a grown woman, and I'm in no position to ask questions. But after everything that happened, I do not like not knowing where you are."

I deflate. "I know, Dad, but it's complicated."

"Do you have a boyfriend? Does Pip? Is that why my girls aren't coming home at night?"

"The short answer is yes. I've been staying with my boyfriend." I silently add the s.

"That's wonderful, Lambchop. When do I get to

meet him?" He sounds genuinely happy, and I'm slightly taken aback.

"Uh…" Holy crapola! How do I deal with this?

After I don't say anything for a full minute, my father sighs again. "I understand you are ashamed of me. I haven't been a great father and I have no right intruding on your life now that you're an adult, but I'd like us to be closer, which means meeting the man you're staying with night after night. I mean, you never stayed the night when you dated Matt. Not even after you got engaged. To be honest, I hated that little peckerwood. His family is the worst."

I giggle. My father never said boo-hiss while I was dating Matt. I surely never told him why I broke off the engagement, and he never asked. "Let me contact Pip and I'll call you back with dinner plans. Okay?"

"Okay," my father agrees. "I'll be waiting for your call."

The line goes dead and I immediately dial Pip. She answers on the second ring. "Hey there."

"Dad's been trying to contact you."

"I know. It's so weird to have him call so often."

I roll my eyes. "He wants to have dinner."

"Well, I'm out of town right now…"

"When do you get back?"

"Saturday night."

"Okay. So, Sunday night?"

"That's fine. I'll make it work." Pip giggles, letting me know she's not really paying attention to me.

"There's something else," I hedge.

She must pick up on my discomfort, because her tone becomes a lot more focused. "What's wrong?"

"Dad asked if I had a boyfriend."

She laughs. "Did he now? What did you say?"

"Yes."

"And what did he say?"

"When can I meet him?"

Pip's voice muffles, and I can hear her walking away from the TV and presumably the men watching it with her. "You know, our men don't think very highly of Walter."

"I know."

"Nothing good can come from telling him about our relationships."

"But he's not going to stop asking about my whereabouts after everything that happened. He's trying, Pip. I know you aren't ready to forgive him, but I can't turn my back on him. He's our father."

She sighs, and I imagine, also rolls her eyes. "Blah."

"What are we going to do?"

I listen to silence for a good thirty-seconds before she says, "You talk to your men and I'll talk to mine and we'll discuss this tomorrow. Until then, tell Dad we'll have dinner Sunday night."

"Okay."

"Love you, Leti."

I smile. I love hearing her say that to me. "Love you too, Pip."

"What's going on?" Caiden slides his arms around me and kisses the top of my head.

I shake my head. "Let me make this phone call real quick and then I need to talk to you—all of you."

He looks me in the eye, trying to read me like they always do, and then nods, placing another sweet kiss against my forehead. "We'll be in the kitchen waiting for you."

I call my dad back and let him know that Sunday night for dinner works, but I can't confirm the headcount.

Then I lay my eyes on my three men watching me from the kitchen, warmth infusing my bones as I recognize the genuine concern they have etched in their features. These men love me. They'll do anything to make me happy. But this might be the biggest thing I'll ever ask them to do, because Pip is right—our men do not think much of our father.

"I can't believe we're doing this," Reese grumbles from the passenger seat.

Caiden snorts while Soren shrugs from the seat beside me. "It'll be fine."

"Will it?" I rub my palms on my pants. I'm sweating, literally sweating, as we drive around the property to meet Pip and her men at her apartment in the back. My father expects us at six, but we're meeting at five to go over our game plan.

We've never spent time together. Heck, I've never met her men before.

My sister and I see each other at least once a week.

The guys see each other in the office.

But we've never hung out as couples.

Trouples?

Quadrouples?

What the hell are we?

Now I'm sweating even more as I realize I have no idea what you call this—besides love.

Throwing the Suburban into park, Caiden turns around in his seat to face me. "Of course it will be. Your father may love you, but he didn't take care of you for a long ass time. We love you and we want to take care of you forever. If he doesn't approve of us, fuck him. If you need his approval to love us—" he looks to Reese and then Soren "—then we have a problem I'm willing to move heaven and earth to fix. I personally don't need Walter's approval, but I'm willing to try to have a relationship with him to make you happy. This is for you and only you because we love you."

Reese tilts his head in Caiden's direction. "What he said."

I giggle and shake my head. "I love you, too, and although his approval did matter to me at one time, if he makes me choose tonight, he will lose. I will always choose you."

"Then it's settled. Let's go meet Dad." Reese chuckles. "Again."

They escort me out of the vehicle and through Pip's front door, which is wide open. Three men, big and wide, with a thin military veneer like my men, sit in the living room. They stop talking and stand, nodding their acknowledgments to Reese, Caiden, and Soren.

One man steps forward and offers me his hand. "Nice to meet you, Leti. I'm Lee."

I blush—I have no idea why—as I give him my hand. "Hi."

He jerks his thumb over his shoulder. "These are my partners, Case and Porter."

They both step forward and offer me their hands. I shake them before being pulled back into Caiden's protective embrace.

Porter glances from me to Caiden and chuckles before taking his seat.

"Where's Pip?" I glance around.

"She's in her room, changing clothes," Lee says.

"Again," Case adds with a shake of his head.

"Hi!" My sister comes bouncing out of the bedroom in a cute, flirty dress that hits mid-thigh. She wraps her arms around me and pulls me out of Caiden's arms. After going a lifetime without her touch, I have to say, my sister gives pretty darn good hugs.

"Hey," I squeak, surprised by her exuberance.

"We didn't really meet last time." She thrusts her hand out, forcing Reese to take it. "I'd like to say I wasn't quite myself, but I think we all know that would be a lie."

Lee shakes his head and grabs her arm, pulling her to him. "Pet, this is Reese, Caiden, and Soren." He points to each of my men.

"Now that we've been introduced—" she claps her

hands together "—who wants tequila shots before the big meet and greet?"

I watch our men exchange knowing looks and I realize my sister is a lot more nervous than she lets on. "I don't think we should drink before meeting with Dad."

"Agreed, sweetheart," Case takes the tequila bottle out of her hands.

I sink into Caiden's embrace and glance up at my men. "Have you ever met someone's parents before?"

They shake their heads. "You're the only woman we've ever loved, baby."

I glance over at Pip's men. "Have you?"

More shaking of heads.

"So, this is new for everyone?"

"Fuck it." My sister throws her hands in the air. "Let's surprise Dad and arrive early."

I swallow the lump in my throat and sag into Caiden's chest. "Might as well get this over with."

We walk as a unit over to the house, Pip and I walking hand in hand with our men following behind us. The tension is thick, and I'm regretting not doing this by ourselves. We should have presented our life choices to our father without six large, testosterone-laden, possessive, intimidating, gun-toting men standing behind us.

This is going to be a disaster.

"Girls!" Our father opens his arms, a genuine smile lighting up his face. "I'm so happy—"

His smile falls and his eyes narrow as they land on our men behind us. "What are you doing here?"

"Mr. Krushner." Reese nods his head in acknowledgement, his hands clasped in front of him.

My father's gaze bounces between them, the wheels turning in his head. "What's going on?"

I don't know where my bravado comes from, but I'm the first one to speak. "You wanted to meet our boyfriends."

"Which one?" My father's face contorts with true confusion.

"Uh."

"Well..." Pip breaks free from her temporary state of paralysis. She grabs Lee, Case, and Porter and pulls them over to one side. "These three are mine, and those are Leti's."

Our father stares at the men and shakes his head. "What?"

She speaks slower, enunciating each word. "I'm. Dating. These. Three. Men. Leti—"

I sigh. "Pip."

"What?" she snaps.

Shaking my head, I turn to Reese, Caiden, and Soren. "I screwed up. I shouldn't have dragged you into this."

"Baby," Caiden cups my cheek. "We are here to support you, but we are also here to stand up for us."

"You're dating three men?" my father says from behind me. "At once?"

I glance over my shoulder and cast a small smile. "Yes."

He points to Pip and then to me. "You're dating the men I paid to secure and rescue you?"

My sister and I nod.

"I'll have your jobs!" he stammers and glares over our heads.

Lee shrugs. "You are certainly entitled to submit a complaint."

"Daddy, we didn't start dating until after we were home and the case was closed. You can't do shit about their jobs." Pip smiles, pulling out her manipulative sing-song voice I haven't heard her use in years.

Our father narrows his eyes. "If you continue with these torrid relationships, I'm cutting off your trust funds. They're only interested in you for *my* money."

My sister laughs. "I have my own money."

I sigh and shake my head. "They didn't know about our trust funds. It never came up." Plus, he can't do anything with our trust funds because our mother set them up when we were children and they come to term on our twenty-fifth birthdays, regardless of our relationship with our father.

Still, the topic of money has never come out of Reese, Caiden, or Soren's mouth. I've practically lived with them for three months and they've never asked me to pay a bill, buy food, nothing.

Reese shakes his head. "Mr. Krushner, you're making a huge mistake. You lost too many years of your daughters' lives and are only now reconnecting with them. Do you really want to go to war with us because you can't wrap your mind around our unconventional relationship? We understand this isn't standard, but I promise you will never find men more dedicated to loving and protecting your daughters."

My father shakes his head. "It's impossible."

Caiden speaks up. "It's improbable, but not impossible, and actually quite common in our world."

I take a step forward, grabbing my father's undivided attention for the first time in a long time. "Nothing you say is going to change how I feel about my men. I love them, and they love me. If you can't accept that, I have no choice but to understand. However, while nothing you say will change how I feel about them, everything you say will affect how I feel about you. I don't need your blessing to have my happily ever after. I already have it, and I'm never letting it go."

"Nicely said." Pip holds her hand up for a high five.

I frown and shake my head at her.

Lee snatches her hand out of the air and pulls her into his arms.

Our father watches this exchange and runs his hands down his face, looking thoroughly exhausted. "I don't want to fight with you. I had to fight with your grandparents when I fell in love with your mother, or more to the point, when she fell in love with me. In their eyes, I was never good enough for her because I didn't come from the right family. I swore I would never do that to you."

His eyes bounce around the room, although he no longer looks directly at us. He shakes his head. "This is too much for me to process right now. I need time to think about my feelings, so I may choose my words more carefully next time we speak. If you'll excuse me, I will skip dinner this evening."

My father turns and walks up the stairs a shell of a man, much like I have known him most of my life. My mouth hangs open and tears well in my eyes as I watch him retreat.

Reese pulls me into his arms.

Pip smiles and rubs my arm comfortingly. "It's going to be okay. Let's go out to dinner, the eight of us."

"I think I'd rather go home." I try to force a smile in return. "But we should have dinner soon."

Caiden rubs my back while Soren interlaces his fingers with mine. "Let's go home, baby."

The eight of us walk to my sister's apartment in silence. We say our cordial goodbyes and are driving down the road less than ten minutes later, exiting the neighborhood I grew up in and on the highway to the north end of Chicago.

"How are you feeling, doll?" Reese finally says.

"Foolish." I cast my eyes to the ceiling to hold back the tears. "I don't know why I thought—"

"Baby girl. Your eternal optimism is one of the things we love about you." Caiden winks at me through the rear-view mirror.

Soren slides his hand up my thigh. "Honestly, beautiful, that conversation went a lot better than I expected. Your father loves you, and he's going to come around because Reese told him exactly what he needed to hear. He's not going to lose his connection to his daughter over her relationship with us as long as we keep her safe and happy."

I blink, causing a rogue tear to fall down my cheek. "Do you think so?"

Reese turns around and smiles at us. "I finally said something smart, huh?"

"It was bound to happen, eventually." Soren grins and lifts my hand to his lips. "How about we grab a pizza, go home, and watch Scooby-Doo?"

Smiling, I look up at them through my lashes. "I have a better idea."

"What's that, doll?" Reese arches his brow as Caiden brings the car to a stop in front of the garage.

"You make love to me."

Caiden grins, looking over his shoulder and throwing the Suburban into park. "We can do that, baby."

My men bought and renovated a six-unit apartment building less than ten miles from the Navy Pier a couple of years ago—turning it into a massive, yet understated house in the Belmont neighborhood. From the outside, it looks nice and respectable, but no one would ever suspect what kind of hi-tech stuff they have going on inside. Because it looks like an apartment building, complete with faux doors and empty mailboxes, the metal fence surrounding the property feels normal. None of the neighbors know the amount of surveillance they are under every time they walk down the street, past the house.

The metal security gate closes behind us, and Soren offers me his hand as he exits the backseat. I scoot across and he lifts me into his arms, carrying me into the house and straight into our bedroom, leaving Caiden and Reese to lock up behind us.

I giggle. "Ready to play?"

"I'm ready to get you out of your head, beautiful."

"I'm fine. Truly."

His brilliant blue eyes sparkle as he smiles. "I love you so damn much, Leti. I don't want you to regret choosing us."

"I won't."

"You know, if you ever want to quit your job..." Soren looks over his shoulder at the same time as Reese and Caiden walk into the room. "I mean, if working with your father proves painful, we will take care of you."

"We'll always take care of you, doll." Reese cups my face and kisses me.

"I'm sorry I never told you about the trust fund." I know that's what this is about. My father's words were a slap to their faces—and a slap to mine.

"There's nothing to tell us." Caiden shakes his head as he unbuttons his shirt. "Your money is yours. As you know, we do quite well for ourselves and don't need your money."

I shake my head and chuckle. "I can't believe he—"

"It was a logical jump for a man in his position to make," Soren says, brushing my hair off my neck and kissing my shoulder as he circles around to my back. "He came from nothing and worked his ass off to build his empire. He doesn't know us, and I'm sure he would be suspicious of anyone who didn't come from his world."

"But if he knew you, he'd know the idea is ridiculous."

Soren grips the ends of my shirt and pulls it over my head, tossing it to the floor before reaching around my waist and unbuttoning my jeans. He slides his hands down the front of my underwear, the tip of his finger going straight to my clit, causing me to moan.

"Beautiful?"

"Yes?" I lean my head back on his shoulder.

"It's time to get you out of your head." He kisses me while vibrating his finger in tiny circles.

Reese pulls his shirt over his head and kicks off his shoes while undoing his belt. He steps forward and unzips my jeans, pulling them and my panties down my legs as he kneels in front of me. "It's also time to eat this pussy."

He pulls one of my legs up and drapes it over his shoulder, pressing his mouth and flicking his tongue against my labia. Rubbing his face, he buries his mouth between my folds and laps his tongue across my pussy, bumping my clit and building my pleasure until I can't help but roll my hips.

Soren wraps his arms around me, supporting and leaning me back so that Reese can spread me wide and plunge his tongue deeper. He snaps open the clasp on the front of my bra and Caiden peels the cups from my breasts.

"What a good girl. Our personal buffet." Caiden bends forward and sucks my nipple into his mouth while Soren nuzzles my neck and rolls my other nipple between his thumb and forefinger. My men are amazing, knowing exactly how to touch and stimulate me everywhere at the same time.

"Oh, god," I moan, my climax teetering on the edge.

Soren puts his mouth on my ear. "You know what we want to hear."

As time goes by, my men, specifically Soren, coax me into talking dirty to them, using the words they use when talking to me in the bedroom. Things I couldn't say to myself in my head three months ago, I now say aloud to them.

"I'm going to come," I pant, letting loose with the words.

"Come for us, baby," Caiden says, biting my nipple and sending me over the edge.

I explode onto Reese's tongue, flooding his mouth with my release. He growls, drinking his fill, sucking on me until the tremors shaking my legs stop. "Fuck, I love how you come."

Soren lifts me in his arms and carries me to the bed. Caiden crawls up my body, kissing me from navel to neck, lavishing attention to my breasts as Reese and Soren finish undressing. Caiden rolls us until I'm straddling his waist and slides his cock inside my wet and wanton cunt. My eyes roll back and I press my palms on his chest as I ride his impressive length.

Gone are the days where I'm shy in the bedroom. They've never once denied me, or embarrassed me about what brings me pleasure. We've even delved into blindfolds and restraints—my men tying me up with their silk ties the last time we went to The Access Club.

Reese climbs onto the bed next to us, fisting his cock. He doesn't have to say anything. I open my mouth and silently ask him to take his pleasure. He caresses my cheek with his thumb. "That's my girl."

Caiden slides his hand between us, placing his thumb over my clit, amping up the friction. I moan around Reese's cock, rolling my hips harder and faster while my men caress me with gentle fingers and precious kisses.

Seconds later, Soren is behind me, his lube-slicked finger sliding down my ass crack and circling my puckered hole. I lean forward on my elbows, arching my back and offering him access. Reese slides down with me while Caiden grips my hips, as if we've practiced this a million times and are trained to move together with fluid-like grace.

We haven't done this a million times, but I'd be lying if I didn't say I wasn't addicted to them, desperate for them, and take them as often as possible. We also have sex individually, or sometimes there are three of us versus four. It really depends on who is around, and considering I can't keep my hands off them, we always make it work.

I am constantly surprised by the lack of jealousy between them—but god forbid another man looks at me or a woman smiles at one of them. I try to hide my jealousy, but my men don't hide an ounce of their possessiveness.

Considering their size and intensity—any man who gives me a second glance backs off quickly.

Outside of our relationship, I'm still the same old wallflower. I'm learning to stand up for myself at the office, and considering my father takes notice of me now at work, others are learning not to talk over me.

"Are you ready for me, beautiful?" Soren places a kiss on the small of my back.

I answer by arching deeper and thrusting my ass in the air, my hand wrapped around Reese's erection as my ride on Caiden's cock slows down.

He growls as he pushes past the tight ring of muscle and slowly sinks his cock into my ass. "What a good girl."

Caiden takes over, his fingers wrapped around my hips as he slides in and out of me.

I focus my attention on Reese, hollowing my cheeks and taking him in as deep as I can. He cups the back of my head, pumping his hips, thrusting his cock past my lips, chasing his own release. "Ah, doll. You suck my cock so well."

My clit rubs against Caiden's thumb as they scissor in and out of me, one man pushing as the other pulls, keeping me thick and full and on the verge of exploding. My inner walls clamp down as my orgasm builds, and electricity runs through my limbs.

"Are you going to come for us, baby?" Caiden thrusts hard and fast into me at the same time as Soren buries himself deep and shoots his load, causing my orgasm to break free. My pussy pulsates, milking Caiden's cock. He groans, latching onto my nipple as he also comes.

"You fuckers," Reese growls, wrapping his fingers around mine and jerking himself to completion. I swallow his cum until he's depleted, and he falls back on his ass. "Holy shit, doll. I will never get enough of you."

Soren pulls out and wraps his arms around my waist, rolling me off Caiden to lie between them. Caiden turns to his left and flashes me a lazy smile. "Hey, baby."

"Hi." I bite my lip, a small blush hitting my cheeks. No matter how carnal we are in the middle of it, I always get a wave of bashfulness afterwards. What does that mean?

He chuckles, like always, and runs his fingers over my breast. "Is that what you had in mind when you asked us to make love to you?"

"Yes."

"But you want more, don't you?"

I giggle. "Yes."

Soren nuzzles my neck. "I love how you never get enough of us, beautiful. You're insatiable."

"I know. Is there something wrong with me?"

"Not as far as we're concerned."

"How could one man satisfy a woman?"

The smile on Caiden's face falls. "You don't ever have to worry about that. It's you and us, forever."

Soren and Reese get up, leaving me and Caiden to snuggle in each other's arms. Reese throws on some pants and goes to the kitchen while Soren runs us a bath. A few minutes later, Reese walks in with my phone in his hand. "You have quite a few missed calls. Your phone was beeping in your purse."

I glance at my phone. There is one missed call from my father, along with three missed group text messages. Blowing out a breath, I open my messaging app.

> My girls. I'm sorry for the way I responded to you and your gentlemen. The idea of my daughters being serious with any man, much less three men, is a lot to take. I've spent the last few hours wondering what your mother would say about this?

> After much reflection, I realized she'd tell me the only thing that matters is that our girls are loved, protected, and happy. I know you are protected. These men are the best of the best, which is why I hired them. Over the last few months, you have certainly seemed happy. I thought it was because of our new relationship, which I suppose was my ego making a fool of me. If you are truly loved, then I have no choice but to find a way to accept this.

Please give me time and have faith in
me. I do not want to lose the progress
we've made building our relationship.
Could the three of us have dinner next
week? I would like to talk this out as a
family. I love you girls.

I sigh and put down the phone. My father is trying, but I wonder if Pip will agree? There was more emotion in this text message than I saw from him for ten years, and I have to believe he meant every word.

"Everything okay?" Caiden rubs his thumb over the lines on my brow.

"Yeah. I think it will be." I smile.

Because I am loved.

I am protected.

And I'm beyond happy.

Want more? Check out the Bonus Epilogue available to newsletter subscribers.

If you haven't already, be sure to read Our Bratty Queen, the companion to Our Wallflower Queen. Skip forward a couple of pages to get the blurb and link.

ENTES TUERE
PUNIRE IMPIOS

REESE

It's only seventy-five degrees with a cool, light breeze on the beach, and yet I'm sweating my balls off.

Am I nervous? No, not really. But I don't like being looked at, and as of right now, as we stand up waiting for our bride to make her way down the aisle, all eyes are on us.

At least I'm sharing the spotlight with my brothers.

Porter snorts and I turn to find Caiden making funny faces at the trio of men standing across from us, waiting for their own bride—the spitting image of our Leti—to walk down the aisle. I smack his arm and shrug in Lee's direction.

"What?" Caiden chuckles and pulls on the buttons of his shirt as if to fan himself. Thank god Leti and her sister didn't require us to wear suits. One, it's too fucking hot. Two, sliding on a tie and then sporting a hard-on mid-ceremony while Leti's father and all of our old unit members look on would have made this even more uncomfortable. Unlike the group standing across from us, we haven't had a civil ceremony yet. Currently, there is no piece of paper legally binding one of us to Leti.

When the time comes, it will most likely be me, although it could be any of us.

Why do I think it should be me?

After I took a baseball bat to my mother's boyfriend at the ripe age of twelve, I spent the next few years in and out of the system whenever my mother fell into another relationship with a guy who didn't like to be challenged. After the last time, when I was old enough to be emancipated, I cut ties with my mother and haven't talked to her since.

It's been fifteen years.

You can't save someone who doesn't want to be saved, and I spent all my formative years trying to save my mother, who only wanted to be coveted by a man.

Always the wrong man.

Effectively, I have no family. Caiden's and Soren's family stories aren't much better. I guess we'll need to decide when the time comes.

Leti's father Walter—well, I don't think he'll ever call any of us son, which none of us want anyway, but he's not a dick, and that's all that matters. We haven't had a ton of interaction with him—a couple of family dinners which are always interesting—but that's about it.

We decided we'd do this ceremony first, all of us joined as one before we deal with the paperwork, which doesn't mean dick in the long run. Legally, we've already updated our wills and property records to include Leti—not that she needs anything we can offer her financially. But that's not the point. It's our job to protect and provide for her, and that's what we will do, always.

Prince's "Sexy Muthafucker" plays, causing all our heads to snap up. My eyes go directly to the men across from us, because Leti would never choose a song that drew additional attention. Hell, she wouldn't have chosen any of this. Even though she hasn't admitted it, we know this is all Epi trying to make up for lost time—years where she wasn't sharing experiences with her twin sister. Lee's face turns red and his eyes are on the ground as he slowly shakes his head. It's odd to be at the front of the line, technically subject to the same scrutiny, and know none of the attention belongs to you. I chuckle and elbow Caiden at the same time as he points at them and laughs. "That's definitely for you."

Leti and Epi walk out of the bridal suite in similar dresses tailored to meet their individual styles. Epi's is tight and short and leaves little to the imagination. Even though I trust all the men assembled here with my life, I wouldn't want to be Lee, Case, or Porter right now. I wouldn't want twenty virile, dominant men looking at my bride-to-be with anything other than a brotherly gaze—although, our Leti is so beautiful, it doesn't matter that her dress is a lot more modest with a flared, knee-length skirt.

She's still stunningly beautiful.

"We are the luckiest fuckers to walk this earth,"

Caiden whispers, with Soren nodding in my periphery to my left.

Leti looks amazing with her hair pinned back from her face, small white flowers adorning her hair. While Epi almost saunters to the beat of the song, Leti has her eyes fixed on us, her chin tilted down—as if she could hide from the eyes watching her.

I flash her a reassuring smile and nod, beckoning her forward with a crook of my finger.

She smiles, close enough now that I can see her eyes as they bounce between the three of us. Her cheeks are rosy red, and it takes everything within me not to jump forward and pull her into my arms, away from the eyes on her—innocent or not.

As if he feels my tension, Caiden wraps his fingers around my forearm. "She's got to do this. It's part of the ceremony."

"I can't believe we agreed to this," I grumble.

"The moment is tense, but the memories will be lovely," Soren adds, and I'm thinking it's the same thing he told her. From the moment we rescued her, he's been the one to calm her the quickest. Possibly because he's the least domineering of us, outside the bedroom.

Inside the bedroom—well, Soren surprises even me, sometimes.

"Hi," Leti squeaks, holding herself rigid to stop from throwing herself into our arms.

I can't help it. I break protocol—if we can agree that a ceremony like this has any protocol—and pull her into my chest, crushing her small bouquet. "Hey doll."

She sags against me, and it's the best feeling in the world.

Caiden and Soren circle around us, each putting a hand on her hip.

"Are we ready to start?" the officiant asks.

"Yeah." I say, without meeting his eye.

CAIDEN

Leti has been a nervous wreck for weeks. Only because we vouched for every person in attendance did she relax and accept her fate, but I have to admit I've been a little resentful of Epi putting her and us in this situation. This is so far outside of Leti's comfort zone that I'm surprised we didn't say no to protect her.

But...

I also understand the undying need to hold on to family. Leti has desired a connection to her sister forever, and now Epi is putting forth a genuine effort to foster, nurture, and grow that bond. Even though I knew this would be hard for her, I couldn't deny her this memory— just like Soren said.

He really is a smart motherfucker, and his people skills have improved immensely since Leti came into our lives. It's like he read a how-to-people manual and then became the Leti whisperer.

Actually, I wouldn't put that past him.

While we have a lifetime of Leti's family ahead of us, my family won't ever be a problem. They disowned me when I left for the military, so although they are still alive and kicking, I haven't dealt with them in years. My parents wanted me to take over the family farm one day, which had been defunct for two generations. They live off of subsidies versus product, but it's a way of life they expected me to embrace.

I wanted more, and I knew I wouldn't find it in Kansas.

But hearing no wasn't something my father handled well, and my mother was in no position to go against him.

So, the day I left for boot camp was the last time I talked to my father. I got one letter from my mother that read *maybe I could come home after I re-assessed my priorities*. I replied with a detailed account of my training as a member of a PsySpecOps unit, outlining the steps my career would take me over the next twenty to forty years of my life.

And that was that.

I accepted the woman I eventually loved would never meet my family long before I knew I'd share said woman with my two best friends.

Long, long before I knew Leti was that woman.

Leti doesn't like it. Family means more to her, even though her family sucked for so long. Initially, she worried she was the reason I would never talk to my family, but after many conversations, she finally under-stood or at least accepted my decision to keep them out —forever.

"Hi." She looks up through her lashes and smiles.

I tuck a loose strand of her hair behind her ear. "You look so pretty, baby."

Lowering her voice, she blushes. "Seems a little silly to wear white, considering what you did to me two nights ago."

"Baby, you will always be pure and innocent to me."

The officiant, a guy named Royal—who also is an ex-PsySpecOps unit member—interrupts us by clapping his hands together, his voice booming to reach the men sitting behind us. "Let's get this boat in the water."

He starts with a joke, some people in attendance laughing... but really, it was a joke for Epi, as I have no doubt any shenanigans pulled today will be her doing alone. I don't mind them. I love a good prank or a gentle tease, but it doesn't turn me on like it does the big baboons across from us.

Thank god for that, too, because I think they have a lifetime of silly string and pink glitter ahead of them.

Leti is more my speed. Someone I can wrap my arms around and care for. Someone who likes to touch and be touched. But someone who also squeals when I manhandle her—lifting her into my arms and demanding she wrap her legs around my waist as I press her back against a door and pound into her.

Yeah, she's about fucking perfect.

"So... this is different." Royal glances between our two assembled groups, his face taking on a more serious note. I barely throw him a look, my gaze fixed on Leti's beautiful face. Traditional marriage never appealed to me. I don't need a piece of paper to do everything within my power to care for her. But I also understand that a legal document between her and at least one of us will help should anything catastrophic ever happen.

Jesus—the idea makes my chest tight.

"Don't take it for granted. Not one damn day.

Cherish your friendship, your bond, your brotherly love, and the love of your woman—the strength of which most people will not experience in their lifetime." I tune back in as Royal ends his little speech, and it's so sweet, I wish I had been listening. He motions to Lee, Case, and Porter with Epi, instructing them to exchange vows.

We can barely hear them, which means the people behind us definitely can't hear a damn thing, which suits me just fine. I rub my thumb over Leti's hand, and lift it to my lips as Royal turns his attention to us.

"Exchange your words of love and devotion, gentlemen."

Reese hooks his finger under her chin and lifts her head so she's looking at him. "Only the gods could have brought you into our lives, and I struggle with my feelings about how we met with where we are now. I hate that you experienced one minute of ugliness, and yet, if you hadn't, we wouldn't be here now. I read something preparing for today. It said: The most beautiful things grow out of filth, shit, and darkness. So I guess that sums us up. We might have pulled you from filth, but you pulled us out of the darkness. You are the beacon of light that guides us every day. You try to be invisible, but your light is beautiful and blinding, and you'll never be able to hide from us."

Damn, that was impressive. I didn't realize Reese had those words in him.

Soren goes next. "They diagnosed me with a learning disability at a young age and treated me like an outsider my entire life. When I joined the military—which I believed was my only opportunity to change my trajectory—I spent all of boot camp thinking I'd made a horrible mistake. Then I got recruited out of AIT and put into a team with my brothers standing with me today. They gave me my first taste of family, but you, Leti, are what makes our family home. You complete the empty parts of me I never thought I would fill, and I will spend my last breath making sure you are protected, loved, and happy."

"Hey, baby." I smile down at her, all the words I prepared dying before they can leave my tongue. She's a vision, perfect in every way, and words are stuck in a lump in my throat.

She smiles with tears in her eyes. "Hi."

I shake my head. "Fuck, I love you more than I thought was possible to love another person. My brothers have said everything I want to say, but better. You are our everything. We thought we were living life before we met you, but now I realize we were biding our time, waiting for you. Thank you for trusting us, believing in us, and loving us. We'll never take you for granted, but will remind you every day that you are the center of our world."

LETI

I can't stop the happy tears falling down my cheeks, and I know my men are doing everything they can to not wrap me in their arms and shelter me from the onslaught of emotion flowing between us. They are so protective, so loving, and want only absolute joy and happiness for me.

I know there are people watching us, but there is no way they can hear us. My men have talked to me, their words meant only for me, and the rest of the people fade away as I'm pulled into the love between us.

"I can't believe I'm here right now, surrounded by more love than I ever dreamed of when I was young and fantasizing about meeting a knight in shining armor—one who would rescue me from the castle tower high above the keep. My knights, all three of them, showed up in black Kevlar, but nonetheless shined for me. You understood me immediately, always anticipating what I need and giving me what I want. No woman has ever been gifted a love more perfectly suited for her. I'm lucky my sister shares a similar bond, otherwise I don't know if I would have been strong enough to accept your love. Now, I know I wouldn't have survived without it. My vow to you on our wedding day is to never apologize for how much I love, cherish, or desire you. I'm the luckiest girl in the world, and I'm not sorry for being greedy—unwilling to let you go. I love you."

From behind me, Royal says. "Truly beautiful. I had no idea you guys had such poetry within you."

"Fuck off," Reese grumbles without lifting his eyes from me.

Smiling, I tsk and shake my head at him.

"Now that's the kind of balladry I expect," Royal laughs. "Exchange your rings, if you have them."

I pull from my dress pocket three identical black titanium rings that remind me of them in their tactical gear. "I didn't get you individual rings, although each of you is unique to my heart. You each fill a particular void, and yet, I can't prioritize one void over the other. I love all of you the same, and yet different, and when I tried to make sense of my feelings, I found myself even more confused by the thoughts running through my brain. I had to accept the fact that you complete me, you complete each other, and together we are perfection."

Reese leans forward and kisses me, before sliding his ring onto his finger. "I love it."

"And you." Caiden leans forward and kisses my cheek.

Soren pulls a ring from his pocket. It's tri-gold with a black band. "We thought you would like this ring, which is like the one the guys are giving your sister right now. It's a puzzle ring with four interlocking pieces which represent the four of us. Apart, one piece is incomplete, but together, they are perfectly aligned."

"It's beautiful." I cup his cheek and kiss him. "I love it."

The officiant clears his throat behind me. "With the vows and rings exchanged, and the sun setting behind us, in front of your friends and family, and under the blessings of the gods, I pronounce you family. Brides, take your husbands."

The men behind us laugh—hooting and hollering—and I can only assume Epi and her men are doing something outlandish.

"Come on." Reese holds out his hand and escorts me toward the water's edge, Soren grabbing my other hand while Caiden walks in front of us. We are far enough away now that I can't hear anything except the water lapping at the sand. Reese spins me into his chest, claiming my lips in a way that has me melting against him. "You're my wife now."

"Our wife." Caiden pulls me out of Reese's hands and lifts me in his arms. I have no choice but to wrap my legs around his waist as he kisses me as deep as Reese, but with the added sensation of feeling Caiden's hard cock pressed against the softest, hottest part of me.

I moan as Soren comes up behind me, his chest pressed against my back.

The sun drops below the horizon in the distance, masking us in a faint darkness that emboldens me as I clutch at my men.

Soren kisses my neck, his fingers inching up my skirt. "We plan to fuck our wife all weekend, but for now, I want to put that dazed look on your face as we toast our nuptials with our guests." He slides his hand between my legs, pressing the tip of his middle finger against my clit as Caiden continues to kiss me senseless. I ride his finger—out of my head in seconds as I hear nothing but words of love and devotion from my husbands.

My husbands.

The thought breaks my orgasm free. Just a small one, but enough to turn me into molten goo surrounded by all three of them.

"That's our girl," Reese growls, pressing a kiss against the side of my neck as Caiden lowers my feet to the sand.

"Can you handle an hour or two mingling with our guests?" Soren asks. "Because if not, I'll take you to our cabana right now."

"The fuck you will." Caiden shakes his head, a sly grin spreading his lips. "I know what you're trying to do. If she goes, we all go."

I giggle. "I'm fine with mingling."

Reese smooths down my dress and offers me his hand. "Let's go, wife."

SOREN

I never thought I'd face the men from the PsySpecOps division while holding the hand of my wife.

Our wife, but also my wife, too.

"Congratulations." Garrett walks up with a cute redhead under his arm, Xander and Darian not far behind them.

"Thanks." I shake their hands and then introduce Leti to all of them.

"Nice to meet you, Leti." Xander smiles and nods, placing his hand on the back of their female. "This is Carlisle."

"Hi." Carlisle smiles, a slight blush hitting her cheeks as she shakes Leti's hand. She's wearing a maxi dress and has the smallest baby bump pushing against the silky fabric, pulling my gaze down and then up to make eye contact with Garrett, who gives me a self-satisfied waggle of his brow.

I throw him an imperceptible nod of congratulations, but say nothing. I don't want to embarrass his female and draw awareness to her or her condition when I suspect she doesn't enjoy being the center of attention anymore than my Leti does. "How's business in New York?"

"It's good. Busy enough to keep the cash flowing, but

not so busy we can't take breaks when we want to. It's a gentle balance, not growing too big, you know?"

"I can understand that. How does Victor feel about you? Has he said hello?"

Darian shrugs. "He's been cordial, but it's obvious he's still butt hurt. He'll get over it."

Epi runs up and pulls Leti out of my hands, dragging her into a strong sisterly hug. Then, to my surprise, she releases Leti and throws her arms around me. "Thank you, Soren. I know this is the worst thing you can imagine doing, ever, so thank you for doing this for her—and for me."

I give her a gentle pat on her shoulder, unbelievably uncomfortable with her affection. "Anything for Leti— and for you. I guess you're my sister now."

She pulls away and grins. "That's right. I now have three new brothers-in-law to annoy."

"Pip," Leti chides.

"I'm kidding." She smacks my shoulder at the same time as Case swings her in a circle before setting her down with his arms wrapped around her waist.

"Is she planning shenanigans?" He smiles, shaking the hands of the men from the Delta-3 team.

I shake my head. "None that I've heard of yet."

"Well, if you do hear of any, let me know. We're keeping a tally for later."

Epi gasps. "Case!"

"What? It's not like every person here doesn't know by looking at you that you're the troublemaker of the group."

Porter and Lee walk up behind them with Reese and Caiden, who hand me a beer. "What are we talking about?"

"Silly string." Case and Porter exchange a look that tells me there's more to this story.

Epi huffs and turns her attention to Carlisle. "Hi, I'm Epi."

"Hi."

"Let's go meet the other ladies." Epi takes both Carlisle and Leti's hands and drags them away without a second glance at any of us.

"Uhhh..." Garrett says, temporarily stunned.

"Yeah, that just happened." Porter nods and tilts his bottle, taking a long draw off his beer. "She's a handful, but she means well."

We watch as our brides approach the blonde and brunette with Ken, LeRoux, Paddy, Stiles, Bastion, and Romeo. By the way the blonde jumps up and down, I'm assuming her energy is more on Epi's level than Leti or Carlisle's. The brunette kisses Bastion's cheek and then leaves with the ladies, who giggle on their way to the bar.

"This is fucking insane," Xander says. "Did anyone ever think we'd be together again? And for a wedding?"

"No," a chorus of rumbles concurs.

The Tennessee guys join us, shaking hands and clinking beer bottles. Soon, multiple conversations are going on at once, and like always, I'm standing on the periphery as a spectator, even though none of the guys actively exclude me.

Romeo comes around and greets me. "Congratulations, Soren. Glad to see you found a good one."

"Thanks. Who's the brunette?"

"That's our Evelyn. I think she and Leti will get along great. They are both shy with crazy female influences in their lives."

"Evelyn?" I search the recesses of my brain. I'm positive Paddy called me about an Evelyn about eight months ago, right after he asked me about a Jimmy—a man that I don't think exists anymore—although I'm smart enough to not ask questions.

"Yeah, it's the one you're thinking about." Romeo's jaw tightens. "But don't ask questions."

"Roger. Is the blonde her friend?" I don't remember hearing about her.

He nods. "Barbie. Can you believe it?"

Narrowing my eyes, I put it all together. "Barbie and Ken? Paddy and LeRoux?"

Chuckling, he watches the women from across the room like I do. "Hilarious, right?"

"That is funny."

He tips his bottle back, drains the contents, and puts the empty down on a nearby table. "How have you been otherwise? Still programming zeros and ones and making amazing things happen?"

"I'm still playing with my computers." Annoyance builds within me, because I expected some kind of backhanded comment once or twice tonight. I'll admit, I have a chip on my shoulder about my intelligence, especially when surrounded by men who are not only smart, but powerful—skilled and deadly. Even after joining PsySpecOps, I was never as good as them at the physical stuff, and ridicule from my childhood—having my dick knocked into the dirt time and time again—seems to keep that chip on edge.

"I was always jealous of your brain," Romeo says, without looking at me.

"What?" I search his face, looking for any sign of sarcasm.

"Yeah, man. I thought I was smart and then I met you. You intimidated me when we were young, but now that I look back, I kick myself in the ass for not soaking up as much knowledge as possible while I could. I still tinker with electronics in our off time. I would love to run questions by you when I have them."

"Of course. Call me anytime."

Romeo accepts a fresh beer from his partner Bastion, who joins our conversation. LeRoux also joins with Royal, Jayson, and Garrett tagging along.

"This is a damn good thing." Bastion points to the women huddled in the corner. There are five of them, and I'm thrilled to see Leti laughing along with Evelyn. "I imagine falling in love with three men is kind of lonely for them. How many of their girlfriends even know, much less can commiserate? It's good they have this opportunity to meet each other."

"Even if they are comparing notes and making fun of us right now?" LeRoux chuckles.

"Hmmm. I never thought of that," I say. Leti is all I need. She completed our family the moment she arrived, but I never thought about her being outnumbered.

"That's because Leti has her sister, just like Barbie and Evelyn have each other," Romeo says.

Garrett sighs. "Damn, I never thought of that either. Car had practically no family unit when we met her, but I'm sure she'd like someone to bitch about us to when we become too much."

"Which, knowing you, I'm sure, is often." Bastion chuckles and ducks as Garrett takes a playful swing at him.

"Maybe we should have reunions more often? Doesn't have to be a wedding, but a good old-fashioned southern BBQ sounds doable," LeRoux offers as Paddy turns to us, nodding in my direction but saying very little —as is his way. "We're building cabins on the ranch. They should be ready by next year."

"On the ranch." Xander shakes his head and grins. "How the hell did Ken get a Boston boy like you on a horse?"

Paddy shrugs, tipping his beer back.

"How did Darian get a big Midwest boy like you in Manhattan?" LeRoux asks.

"Broadway show tunes. I fucking love them." Xander flashes a predatory smile, daring anyone to follow with shit talk.

No one does.

Everyone continues to talk, grabbing chairs and swapping stories from back in the day when we deployed, talking about things that are still technically classified. I have Caiden sitting on one side of me, Porter on the other, as I sit back and listen to everyone ramble on. There's a familiar energy in the room—lots of testosterone, and yet, it's different—mature and more cautious, as if we all have something (or more to the point, someone) to lose.

And we know it.

Epi and Barbie are natural hostesses, talking to everyone, making sure all are well fed with a drink in their hand. Leti, Evelyn, and Carlisle seem to have found kindred spirits, laughing more than I have ever seen our woman laugh.

"She's happy." Caiden leans forward.

"Truly." I nod, warmth infusing my veins.

"Baby?" Epi plops down in Porter's lap.

"Yes?" He arches his brow, as if he knows some shenanigans are about to come out of her mouth.

"Where's the silly string?" She smiles sweetly and bats her eyelashes.

"Like I'm going to tell you."

She juts her bottom lip. "I know you were the one to find it. If you give them to me, tonight I'll—" She leans forward and whispers in his ear, causing a red-hot flush to creep up his neck.

He closes his eyes and sucks in his breath. "Tonight?"

"As soon as we get back to our cabana." Nodding, she grins in triumph, and something tells me Porter is the weakest link when it comes to giving in to her antics.

"Fine. I'll go get them."

"Eeekkk!" She jumps out of his lap, clapping her hands.

"Lee's going to kill me, but it'll be worth it." He shrugs as he leaves us at the table.

Caiden and I laugh. "Better him than us."

Leti comes over a minute later and sits in Caiden's lap, but puts her legs on mine.

"I had nothing to do with this," she says meekly, snuggling into Caiden's chest.

"Nothing to do with what, doll?" Reese says before he leans down and kisses the top of her head.

I massage her calves, actively reminding myself to keep my hands below her knees. "Silly string, I'm guessing."

Leti's eyes grow wide. "You know about that?"

"Epi's not exactly hiding it." I throw her a wink. "Are you having fun, baby?"

"I am." She beams a beautiful smile. "Evelyn and Carlisle are amazing—I think we'll be lifelong friends. And Barbie is like having another Epi, but a lot more ballsy. Like, I think if a fight broke out right now, she would jump in the middle to defend her men."

I tense. "That would be terrible."

Caiden nods his head. "Yeah, don't you ever do something like that."

"Oh, I'm too much of a wimp to get into a fight." She waves us off.

"That's not true, Leti. I've told you many times, you're one of the strongest women I've ever met."

Caiden interjects. "But if you got into the middle of

one of our fights, you turn it from a simple brawl into a death match, because we'd kill anyone who put their hands on you—even if it was by accident."

"Every man here would do the same for his woman, which means Ken, Paddy, and LeRoux would have to kill every one of us on principle alone."

"Or try to." Reese shrugs, his tone flat as usual.

I don't say what I'm thinking, which is, Paddy and LeRoux have buried more bodies than the rest of us combined. I know I wouldn't want to go against them.

"Jeez. I'm sorry I brought it up." Leti nuzzles her nose against Caiden's jaw and kisses his neck.

"Did you get enough food and drink?"

"Yeah, I'll be ready to leave soon. But first I have to do this thing with Epi." She pulls her legs from my hands and stands, turning to kiss Caiden, and then me.

"Like what? Throw your bouquets?" Reese asks.

She smiles, a blush hitting her cheeks. "Something like that."

"Silly string," Caiden and I say at the same time.

"I love my husbands." She dances away before I can pull her back into my lap.

Porter plops down into the empty seat at the same time the DJ plays music. Epi and Barbie pull Leti, Carlisle, and Evelyn onto the dance floor, but then make another sweep, pulling Phillip, Patty-Ann, and another guy into the middle of the group.

"Who is that?" Xander asks, and I don't have to look to know he's asking about the two men dancing with our women.

"That's the photographer, Phillip, and his boyfriend Danny," Porter says casually. "Trust me. We warned Epi to not poke at anyone's jealousy with this crowd. She almost got Phillip killed once. We don't want a repeat performance of that night."

Even though word of who the two men on the dance floor are spreads quickly, you can cut the tension of the men assembled as they watch their women move their bodies to the beat.

"This is torture," Caiden says, rubbing his hand down his face.

"Leti will be fine," I say, even though I know that's not what he means.

"I'm not worried about her. I'm worried about the Neanderthals surrounding us."

Standing, I stretch my arms over my head. "I know what you mean."

I walk away from the men assembled and the thick tension of protectors watching over their flock, and sit with Walter Krushner, who has spent most of the evening alone. "Hello, Walter."

He looks up from his plate. "Soren."

"Crazy evening, huh?"

A sad smile drifts over his face. "Their mother would have loved this."

"I'm sure she's here with us." I feel the sorrow and grief pouring out of this man. I might never forgive him for how he treated his daughters over the years, but it's obvious he lost himself with the passing of his wife. His love for her was pure and all-consuming, and only now does he realize what he lost by withdrawing into himself for all those years.

Walter smiles and runs a hand through his thinning hair. "She'd be dancing with the girls right now if she was here. She was the perfect combination of Epi and Leti—wild and yet contained. She always knew how to engage people and bring out the best in them without being in their face."

"Leti certainly brings out the best in me."

"You're a good man, Soren. You all are. I couldn't ask for better sons-in-law."

Something about his words wraps their tendrils around my throat in a chokehold, and I stare with Walter as Leti and Epi dance in circles on the floor, crowding in close. It's only then I realize there's a bag in the middle of the dance floor, and all the ladies are jumping up, armed with two cans of silly string each.

I sigh. "Here we go."

Intuition or a sixth sense took me across the ballroom to sit with Walter ten minutes ago. Now I watch the ladies—led by Epi and Barbie—rush the men assembled at a handful of tables on the other side of the room. They spray silly string high in the air, coating everyone to include themselves, laughing and throwing themselves into their men's arms.

"Would your wife have doused you in silly string, too?" I ask.

Walter wipes away a stray tear. "Yeah, she would have."

I smack his hand and stand. "Come on. Let's join the celebration."

PSYSPECOPS
INNOCENTES TUERE
PUNIRE IMPIOS

PsySpecOps soldiers aren't like other soldiers.
They aren't even like other special ops units.
They're a cross of special ops, Intel, EXO, Cyber, and
psychological warfare, to name a few.

Imagine if Chuck Norris, MacGyver, and B.F. Skinner
all jerked off into a test tube and then impregnated
Wonder Woman.
That's would be them.

PsySpecOps doesn't take volunteers. They recruit the
best of the best out of the special forces units.

They are chosen not only for their physical prowess—
marksmanship, hand-to-hand, endurance, strength,
intelligence, instinct, and ingenuity—but also for their
psych profile that says they'll work best as a team.

They're the Army's answer to a super soldier without chemical injections and gamma rays.

Together, the three men psychologically profiled to be a team are a near perfect soldier—accentuating each other's strengths and eliminating any weaknesses.

Rumor has it, ex-PsySpecOps teams prefer to find and share one woman versus date independently. It is said to be an unexpected side-effect of their training.

They functional perfectly as one in all other aspects of their life, so why wouldn't they want to offer the perfect woman a complete package?

The Men of PsySpecOps work hard, play hard, and love hard... all they need is to meet the special woman who can handle all they have to give.

IS THAT YOU?

Men of PsySpecOps
OUR BRATTY QUEEN
KAMERON CLAIRE
USA TODAY BESTSELLING AUTHOR

I'm the bad twin, the loud one, the one dancing on the tables while my critics condemn me. My family rarely knows where I am, much less what kind of trouble I'm starting, which has left me a lonely shell that I fill with my antics.

My sister is my polar opposite in every way. Quiet and in the shadows, she has everyone convinced she's the good twin, but I know better.

When she is kidnapped, my father hires a security team—three hot men who don't find my antics cute in slightest—and suddenly, I want to the good twin.

I want THEIR attention.

I want THEIR discipline.

I want to be under THEIR control.

We were hired by a billionaire to secure and protect his twenty-two year old daughter who is the identical twin of a high-profile kidnapping. As it turns out, our charge—the social media influencer herself—was the intended victim. Now, we're a hundred of miles away in a secluded cabin that is off the grid, which means our princess has no access to her phone, the internet, or her legion of social media followers. She's bored, she's bratty, and she's begging to be put over our knees and spanked.

She's also everything our domineering hearts crave—the one woman who speaks to our primal need to tame her into the perfect little submissive. If this security detail only lasted a few hours, we could ignore her antics and control our needs—but as the hours spread into days, and she ups the ante to include endangering herself, we can no longer avoid what is in front of us.

This brat needs to be tamed.

She's ours to punish, ours to tame, ours to claim as our own.

Our Scrappy Queen

I've been stalked by a guy for months who doesn't under the words: Not Interested. But once he escalates his threat by putting my coworker in the hospital, I decide to go on the offensive and give the creep a taste of his own medicine. As a self-proclaimed control freak, I refuse to live in fear and wait for him to come after me. When I sabotage his wooded torture shack, I accidentally blow up the house and the three-month long investigation belonging to the team that's been watching him instead. Of course, I don't know they aren't his goons when we meet, so our introduction consists of me running, cursing, kicking, and punching, only to ultimately lose the fight, but not before I give one a black eye.

We've been tracking this scumbag for three months, waiting for him to lead us to the big fish—the head of the DiFallo human trafficking empire. But when a hellcat blows up our plans, literally, we scoop her up for questioning. She fights us like no woman ever has before, which unfortunately for everyone involved, only turns us on. Her curves are inviting, her tongue is wicked sharp, and her right hook is a thing of beauty—which makes us want to keep her mouth busy while we tether her hands high above her head.

But when we realize she's the scumbag's victim and not an arsonist on DiFallo's payroll, our protective instincts roar to life.

She says she's not interested in our help, but her actions say otherwise, and although we recognize her skill, we can't leave her to take care of this on her own. Not when we're already convinced she belongs with us.

With her life on the line, she has to give up control to us to survive. When she does…

She's ours to protect, ours to fight for, ours to love.

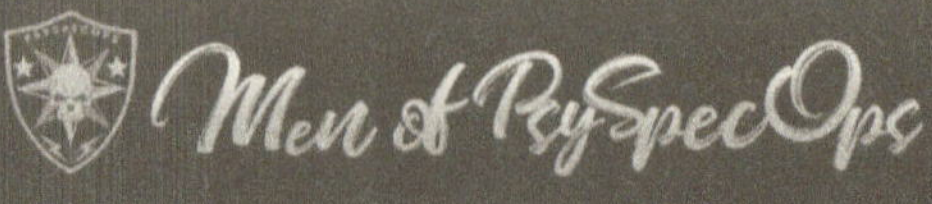

Kameron Claire

USA TODAY BESTSELLING AUTHOR

Our Incognito Queen

She wants her three gorgeous bosses in the dirtiest way. She's forbidden to them, not only because she's their employee, but because she's too pure to be sullied by their darkest desires.

Can one anonymous night sate their needs and fulfill her fantasies?

My bosses are hot, smart, and totally unattainable. But when I glimpse them at The Access Club—New York's hottest underground sex club—and hear a rumor they share their women, I come up with a plan to live out my fantasy, at least for one night.

We have known each other our entire adult life. Bonded since day one of PsySpecOps training, we now own a successful private security business.

We share everything, and we mean, everything. But the one thing we want to share, we can't, because our sweet girl is too pure for the things we want to do to her. We agreed to leave her alone, but when we get a mysterious invitation in the mail, each of us know we're about to get what we want most in this world—her.

One night won't be enough. She's ours to unveil, ours to pleasure, ours to keep.

Also by Kameron Claire

Want more **Witty** Tongues, **Wicked** Needs, & **Wild** Deeds?

Veteran K9 Team

** Military Romance **

Mine to Cherish

Mine to Crave

Mine to Possess

Mine to Adore

Mine to Covet

Mine to Worship

Mine to Protect

Mine to Treasure

Hot Nights with the Boss

** Forbidden Office / Age-Gap Romances **

Dating the Boss

Flirting with the Boss

Teasing the Boss

Tempting the Boss

Rangers Football

Sports Romance

Play Action Fake

Quarterback Sneak

Personal Foul

Two-Point Conversion

Red Zone

Man to Man Coverage

The Men of PsySpecOps

Reverse Harem Romance

Our Bratty Queen

Our Wallflower Queen

Our Scrappy Queen

Our Incognito Queen

Our Enduring Queen (pre-order)

Our Indelible Queen (pre-order)

Our Broken Queen (pre-order)

Our Ageless Queen (pre-order)

Hollywood Lights (Pre-Order)

Billionaire Romance

Show Time (Securing Selyne)

Money Shot

Three Shot

Martini Shot

Long Shot

Grayson Enterprises Series

Bedding the Boss

Enticing the Ex

Tempting the Teacher

Wedding the Widow

Short Story Collections and Bundles

Animal Attraction 4-Story Collection

Vegas Nights 4-Story Collection

Last Stand Saloon 4-Story Collection

Instalove Bundle

Fated Mates of SpecOps Sierra

Paranormal Romance

Riding with the Kodiak

Wild Wolf

Cocky Cougar

Broken Bear

Wanted Wolf

Cursed Cougar

Banished Bear

About the Author

USA Today Bestselling Author Kameron Claire writes stories with witty tongues, wicked needs, and wild deeds. Her paranormal and contemporary books emphasize strong female leads and the protective alpha males who know how to love and support kick-ass, take-charge women. Many of her books contain military veterans, boss babes, dominant men, and goofy K9 hijinks.

Find her everywhere via linktr.ee/kameronclaire
Signed Paperbacks and discounted eBook bundles are available exclusively on her store
Subscribe to the Witty, Wicked & Wild community and read all her books online for as little as $10 a month.

amazon.com/author/kameronclaire

goodreads.com/kameronclaire

bookbub.com/authors/kameron-claire

facebook.com/kameronclaireauthor

instagram.com/kameronclaire

tiktok.com/@kameronclaireauthor

www.ingramcontent.com/pod-product-compliance
Lightning Source LLC
Chambersburg PA
CBHW061345310726
48974CB00001B/211